THE EMPTY DOOR

Clara was gazing at her watch, which seemed to have stopped. It was still twenty minutes to one. There was a small sound like something dropping to the floor, and she raised her eyes in time to see the sealed door swing open, pushed by a brownish hand at the end of an arm clad in faded purple.

It was there only a moment, then it moved aside, then it was no longer in the doorway.

Still watching the empty place where the figure had stood, Clara walked stiffly to the door; there, clinging to the frame, she began to scream wildly.

BANTAM BOOKS offers the finest in classic and modern English murder mysteries. Ask your bookseller for the books you have missed

Agatha Christie

DEATH ON THE NILE
A HOLIDAY FOR MURDER
THE MYSTERIOUS AFFAIR
  AT STYLES
POIROT INVESTIGATES
POSTERN OF FATE
THE SECRET ADVERSARY
THE SEVEN DIALS MYSTERY
SLEEPING MURDER

Carter Dickson

DEATH IN FIVE BOXES

Catherine Aird

HENRIETTA WHO?
HIS BURIAL TOO
A LATE PHOENIX
A MOST CONTAGIOUS GAME
PARTING BREATH
PASSING STRANGE
THE RELIGIOUS BODY
SLIGHT MOURNING
SOME DIE ELOQUENT
THE STATELY HOME
  MURDER

Patricia Wentworth

MISS SILVER COMES TO STAY
SHE CAME BACK

Elizabeth Lemarchand

BURIED IN THE PAST
DEATH ON DOOMSDAY

Margaret Erskine

THE FAMILY AT
  TAMMERTON
NO. 9 BELMONT SQUARE
THE WOMAN AT
  BELGUARDO

Margaret Yorke

CAST FOR DEATH
DEAD IN THE MORNING
GRAVE MATTERS

Margery Allingham

BLACK PLUMES
TETHER'S END
TRAITOR'S PURSE

Elizabeth Daly

THE BOOK OF THE CRIME
EVIDENCE OF THINGS SEEN
THE WRONG WAY DOWN

E. X. Ferrars

MURDERS ANONYMOUS

EVIDENCE
OF THINGS
SEEN

Elizabeth Daly

BANTAM BOOKS
TORONTO · NEW YORK · LONDON · SYDNEY

EVIDENCE OF THINGS SEEN

A Bantam Book / published by arrangement with
Holt, Rinehart & Winston

PRINTING HISTORY

Holt, Rinehart & Winston edition published June 1943
A Selection of Detective Book Club, May 1943
Originally published by Bantam Books in November 1945
Bantam edition / October 1983

PRINTED IN THE UNITED STATES OF AMERICA

H   0 9 8 7 6 5 4 3 2 1

Contents

1 Landscape with Figure   1
2 Research   10
3 Consultation   21
4 No Flowers   32
5 Twenty Minutes to One   41
6 Gamadge Does Not Laugh   50
7 Another Point of View   58
8 Nobody Can Believe It   66
9 Faded Purple   75
10 Foreign Bodies   86
11 Patchwork   95
12 Schemes of Decoration   104
13 Try the Impossible   112
14 An Exorcism   121
15 Line of Inquiry   128
16 The Ladder   135
17 No More Disguise   142
18 Quite Safe Now   149
19 What Money Can Buy   157
20 Gamadge Hears Laughter   162

1

Landscape with Figure

"Mrs. Gamadge, that woman's there again."

Clara looked up from the letter she was writing to her husband. Long shadows from the trees across the road came up the slope of the yard, up to the very edge of the narrow porch on which she was sitting, her feet in rough grass. Clara's face was rosy in the evening light; but the elderly maid, who stood under the branches of a maple at the corner of the cottage, had not all her customary high color.

Clara herself was disquieted, but she had adopted an attitude, and was maintaining it. "Up on the ridge?" she asked, with what seemed no more than mild curiosity.

"Ma'am, she's come down the hill. She's halfway to our wall."

"Then she's on her way here, and we'll find out who she is," said Clara, cheerfully.

"No, ma'am; she just stands there the way she did the other times. First she was up at the edge of the woods, and then she was out on the ridge, and now she's come down the hill. She just stands there and looks at us—in her sunbonnet."

"I wonder where on earth she comes from, and where she's going."

"There's no place for her to come to but here."

"Can't you see her face this time?"

"No, ma'am; the sunbonnet falls together."

"She's just wandering, Maggie; there can't be any harm in her. She *must* be somebody staying at Mrs. Simms', or at the egg-woman's. She's just taking an evening stroll, and of course she's interested in new summer people."

"She doesn't belong at Mrs. Simms', ma'am, and there isn't any such person at Miss Radford's; I told you so before. And how did she get up there on the ridge unless

1

she came through the woods? She never crossed the field; I would have seen her this time and the other times. I didn't see her. I just looked up, and there she was, in that dress and that sunbonnet, looking."

"I only said she couldn't have come through the woods because the trail is miles long—miles!" Clara's voice had risen a little, but she continued more quietly: "Of course I suppose she may have cut through from farther down the highway; I suppose she could get through the underbrush."

"There's not a house for three miles down the highway."

"We don't know all the people around here, Maggie, or why they do things, or where they go. Miss Radford's cows are back there."

"And they came home before this. I don't like the looks of it."

Nor had Clara much liked the looks of it. Six days before, and again three days before, it had stood motionless—a thin figure in faded purple, its limp sunbonnet screening its face—and had looked across slope and hollow at the cottage, just when the sun had begun to sink below the trees across the road.

Clara laid her writing materials on the porch floor, got up, and followed Maggie around the kitchen wing of the house. Far to the right, beyond a broad field, the highway ran east and west; in the angle formed by it and the road to the cottage was a small farmhouse, and another larger one could just be seen among its trees across the way. Behind the cottage a long slope led down to a stone wall, on the other side of which the ground rose steeply to a ridge. Dense woods crowded up to the ridge on three sides, but at one spot the skyline was clear.

A narrow track emerged from the trees on the left, wandered diagonally across the hillside, and disappeared at last into the shadow of the trees on the right. The woman had stood twice on this trail; first at the very entrance to the woods, and then out on the ridge; she was nowhere on it now. There was no figure in the landscape.

Clara, standing in the long grass of the little orchard, gazed to right and left of the trail. "She's gone."

"And I hope she went back where she came from!" Maggie fumbled with her apron. "I hope she's not about the place."

"She went back the other times; walked along the path into the woods. Just like anybody."

"It's her coming closer I don't like."

"Next time I'll go and speak to her. I'll find out who she is."

"You'll not catch her." Maggie followed her employer around to the front of the cottage, which owned no proper back door.

"Probably she'll wait. Probably she'd love to be spoken to. Next time she may come right up to the house."

"I don't want her coming up to the house. She's not right."

Clara stopped to look reproachfully at the old servant who had been with one or another member of the family since Clara was born. "If she were out of her head they wouldn't let her go wandering around!"

"They might, in the country; but that's not what I mean."

down the road, across the way, there ——
egg-woman. But she sells me all kinds of other things too, butter and chickens and things. When you come you'll live in luxury.

I'm glad I didn't bring the animals, though, because the egg-woman has two fierce dogs which would have killed Sun, not to mention Martin. If they ever got loose.

"Your supper is ready, Mrs. Gamadge," said Maggie, coming to the dining room door in a white apron. "And that door to the attic is open again."

Clara, looking a trifle disturbed, gathered up her things. "I suppose there's a draft," she said, "and the old latch works loose."

"There's no draft."

"The door wasn't open when I came down for tea."

"It is now. I was putting your room ready. I saw it when I came up the stairs."

"Please, Maggie, don't bother with my room till the Herons get here with their maid. You have too much to do." Clara went in through the living room, and up an enclosed stairway to a little sitting room on the second floor. The enclosed stairway led on up to an attic, with a landing and a door at the bottom of the last flight; this door undoubtedly stood wide open.

Of course it's wonderful having the Hunters so near. I mean it's only a few minutes' drive up to their place if you go around the mountain. There's a trail through the woods above the cottage—it's called the Ladder, and when you come you'll know why—that goes right up to the ridge they're on; I often walk it—it takes about three-quarters of an hour. I think it was wonderful of Dick Heron to find this lovely place for us all to spend the summer in.

I promised I'd keep you posted about everything, so I'd better tell you that the Herons can't come for two weeks—Tommy had measles, and they have to wait and take him up to his camp. *Now don't worry about it.* I won't be a bit lonely with Maggie here and lots of people dropping in all the time from miles around, and everybody says it's perfectly safe. The car is going splendidly, and I have a telephone.

And I am having no trouble about supplies. Avebury is only five miles off, and the people are obliging; you know

You're just letting her get on your nerves. You're getting lonely here, and you promised you wouldn't. We've been only a week at the cottage, and you're tired of it already."

"Indeed I am not. It's a beautiful spot. You'll have trout for your supper, Mrs. Gamadge; Mr. Craye's man brought them on a string."

Clara said that that would be lovely, sat down on the porch again, and picked up her writing block. Maggie went in by the dining room door. This was a couple of yards from the living room door; if the cottage had no back entrance downstairs it had two front ones, both of which opened on the little roofed verandah. There were other somewhat pleasing anomalies about the house, which had originally been a double one.

Clara went on with her interrupted letter:

... cannot tell you how much I love the cottage. The country is beautiful, and I have nice walks. We have the road to ourselves, nobody travels it but our delivery boys from Avebury, and Gil Craye when he drives over from Stratfield, ten miles off, and the Hunters when they come down from Mountain Ridge, and sometimes my egg-woman. The reason we're so private is that everything to the north for miles is a state reservation—thousands of acres.

Clara looked at it, looked up into the dimness of the attic, stood for a moment with a failing heart, and then slammed the door and latched it; the hasp fell neatly into its slot, and would not be dislodged until she jerked hard at the handle below. She knew it would not; she had gone through the same performance twice before.

The sitting room divided her bedroom from the one which would be the Herons'; she had allotted them theirs because she thought they would like having a bathroom on their landing, but she thought her own the nicest room she had ever had. It was against a hillside, and had two outer doors; one led straight into the woods, the other had its own little porch and rustic stairway, which ended in the grass of the yard. There was something magical about living on two levels at once, something even more magical about going to sleep to the sound of falling water; behind the trees on the other side of the road there were a brook and a waterfall.

The four little windows and the two doors were screened; they could all be open at night. The wallpaper was white and green, the woodwork dark green, the furniture and the four-poster bed painted to match. Clara never entered the room without thinking how much Gamadge was going to like it.

When she was ready for supper she went through the sitting room and the Herons' bedroom, and down a second flight of enclosed stairs to the dining room. This flight went on up to the other attic of the double house, which had been remodeled and ceiled, and in which Maggie slept.

The double nature of the old cottage was again in evidence on the ground floor. Living room and dining room each had a little bedroom attached, as well as its own stairway. Each had its fireplace, once closed up and fitted with a stovepipe, now a neat brick rectangle furnished with andirons. There was a good deal of plain, authentic early American furniture in the cottage; Clara did not understand how the owner could have left it behind—she did not suppose that it had been bought expressly for summer tenants. A bathroom and a kitchen and pantry wing had been built on to the south.

Before sitting down at the narrow dinner table Clara went to the doorway and looked out at the sunset sky. The sky, the trees, the old dirt road—there was nothing else to be seen. So isolated the cottage was, yet so safe! Eli, the head keeper on the reservation, had told her that not in the memory of man had there been tramp or prowler in these parts, so well were they patrolled to the north by the reservation guards. He was an Indian, with the face of a mild Pharaoh, and he had stopped by several times while she was settling in, and sat on the porch with her; had helped her with odd jobs and considered advice. Clara felt much at peace in his company.

She turned away from the quiet scene and sat down at the table. Maggie brought in a dish of broiled trout.

"That's good," said Clara. "I'm starving."

"I wish you'd let me get you regular dinners, ma'am."

"I don't want you to bother until the Herons come, and Mr. Gamadge comes." The last words were spoken with a trace of wistfulness, and Maggie, noticing it, went on more briskly:

"I will say the things that Miss Radford sells us are fine. Broilers no bigger than squabs. That's a nice farm she has, four cows and a horse."

"I suppose she rents the pasture back of the ridge from our landlord."

"She's our landlord."

Clara looked up in surprise. "The egg-woman owns the cottage?"

"And all the property, back to the pond in the woods."

"Well, I never."

"She and her sister lived here till the sister died, last summer. Mrs. Simms told me; she's rich."

"She must be rich, with the cottage, and the farm, and everything."

"No, ma'am, I mean *rich*. The sister left her a hundred and six thousand dollars, and she moved back to the farm. It's the old Radford farm, but it's been rented for years."

"How did the sister come to have so much money, I wonder?"

"It was the sister's husband made it. When he died she came back to live here with Miss Radford. It wasn't fixed up the way it is now, it had no plumbing. The sister was a miser."

"Was she?"

"Yes, and then when she died the bank told Miss

Radford she'd left her the hundred and six thousand dollars. Miss Radford fixed up the farm, and moved in, and then fixed up the cottage. And without Mr. Gamadge and your friends, ma'am, 'tis no place for you."

"Maggie, I'm not going to abandon it for two weeks, after all our trouble getting settled, just because there's no man in the house. It's too silly. Mr. Gamadge might come home any day, and he would love having this place to come to; he hates hotels."

"He'd hate worse for you to be here with only meself to look after you. But what's the poor man to do, off we don't know where, and one of his letters sunk in the sea?"

Clara swallowed some coffee before she replied: "We don't know that it was sunk in the sea, Maggie. It may have got lost. Maggie, it's so pleasant here; I didn't think you'd spoil it for me."

"Ma'am, I'll say no more about it." Maggie went into the kitchen, and returned with raspberries and cream.

After supper Clara took a candle and wandered about, admiring her domain. Miss Radford, she thought, must have engaged excellent decorators. The two principal rooms were done in dark green, the little bedrooms leading off them were in pale green and pale blue, the bathroom was a bright turquoise. All the little windows had white muslin curtains, and the wallpapers had been chosen by experts. Perhaps they had persuaded Miss Radford to leave her valuable pine and mahogany furniture here.

The little pale-green bedchamber off the dining room was to be the Herons' maid's; it was charming. Clara wished that Miss Radford had not had the door in the south wall closed up, though; it was painted to match the woodwork, its latch had been removed and its keyhole plugged. Why should it have been condemned? For warmth in winter, perhaps. Clara wondered whether the egg-woman would let it be opened again, and she also wondered why she had never noticed it on the outside of the cottage.

It must be in that angle where the lilac bush is, she thought, and went back to the living room for her flashlight.

Maggie called to her from the kitchen window: "You're walking out in the wet grass, ma'am?"

"I just want to see where that blind door comes out, Maggie."

She went around the kitchen wing. The lilac bush grew

in an angle between the bathroom and the south wall of the little bedroom; it had been allowed to straggle this year, and its branches almost hid the door, which had no doorstep any more, and which had been painted the yellow of the cottage. It had no knob, its keyhole was invisible; but it was a door just the same, and once the lilac bush had shaded it.

Clara went back to the living room to finish her letter to her husband. He had departed for a destination unknown three months before, and she would not know that he had returned, by plane or by sea, until he was actually on American shores. She wrote:

> Maggie now informs me that the egg-woman I was talking about is our landlady! I wonder if the Herons know? Dick managed the whole thing through an agent in Hartford, and only saw the place once. He fell in love with it, as you will. We can all play golf in Stratfield, and Gilbert Craye wants you to fish with him. The Hunters told Dick there was a cottage for rent this summer; of course they must know. *I* don't know why I fill up space with this! But I shall feel quite silly, giving Miss Radford quarters and dollars for stuff, now that Maggie tells me she has a hundred and six thousand dollars in the bank.
>
> She has an old horse and a buggy, and she brings things to the cottage, but she won't get out and come in. She thinks the horse is very skittish, and she never has a hitching rein. I wanted her to see how pretty everything here is, but it would have been rather a joke on me, wouldn't it, since she had it all done herself? Perhaps she's sick of the sight of it, it must have cost so much. She's a queer, stiff old thing, but polite.
>
> I'm perfectly happy, darling. . . .

At this point Clara stopped writing and bit the end of her penholder. She never knew how to refer to her husband's absence without seeming to lament or complain, and this time also she gave up the problem. She added a few sentences of an intimate and personal nature, and then dated the letter—July 1st, 1942. Gamadge liked dates. She addressed the envelope, as usual, to Washington; an office in Washington got his mail to him in the shortest time and by the shortest way.

It was not until she had reread the letter that the obvious occurred to her. She thought: Can Maggie be as silly as that? put the letter in the envelope, and got a stamp. On her way to the mailbox beside the road she stopped at the kitchen door.

"Maggie," she asked, "did Miss Radford's sister die here—in the cottage?"

Maggie looked up from her dishes. "Why do you want to know that, I wonder?"

"It just occurred to me. I don't know why I vaguely thought before that she was in a hospital. In cities most people do die in hospitals."

"People die where they can, God help them."

"No, but did Mrs. Simms or somebody tell you she died here, and do you mind if she did?"

"Mind? It's not for me to mind such a thing."

Clara, as she went out and came back again, was puzzled by the look that had been on Maggie's face. She had not really spoken as if she minded the simple fact that somebody had died in the cottage, but she had looked as though she minded something else.

The open doorway sent a cheerful fan of light out upon the porch; Clara, standing there, suddenly felt as if she had received a slight, a very slight blow on the chest; she thought: Maggie *can't* be so silly! But she asked Maggie no more questions. She stood breathing in the moist, wood-scented air, and listening to the rush of the waterfall. She stood for several moments after she wished very much to turn and dash into the cottage; but she restrained herself.

"Only a woman in a sunbonnet!" she told herself scornfully, adding: "Besides, she always comes at sunset."

Then she went in and locked both doors. Maggie called: "Will I sleep on the same floor with you till your friends get here, ma'am?"

"Not unless you'd be more comfortable, Maggie."

"Me own room is cool and pleasant enough."

"Then don't think of moving, you're so nicely settled."

Clara took her lamp and went upstairs. The sitting room was cosy and cheerful, the attic door firmly closed as she had left it. Her bedroom welcomed her; the bed was turned down, rambler roses from the porch vine were in a jug on the dresser. She heaped pillows, lighted her reading lamp, and was soon in bed. The waterfall murmured,

an occasional moth struck a window screen with the sound
of a string plucked on a bass viol; this was perfect. But it
would be nice when the Herons came, and they could all
sit and talk in the sitting room before they went to bed.

It's just that attic door that bothers me, she thought. I'll
go up there tomorrow. I'll get Mrs. Simms' man to come
and look at the latch. Of course there's a draft or something.

Clara opened her book, but she could not make herself
read. Instead, her thoughts wandered in and out of the
ambiguous pattern that seemed to be weaving itself about
the cottage, closing it in as a spider web closes around a
leaf; thin as a spider web, and with as little substance. A
woman in a sunbonnet, a door that came open of itself
whenever she appeared; a death, an inheritance, an old
woman who wouldn't come into the cottage.

Clara gave up her attempt to read, put out her light,
and cast her extra pillow on the floor. She lay down in the
dark, and presently she ceased to hear the thrum of moths
against the screens, the sound of the waterfall. The waterfall sent her to sleep.

2

Research

Mrs. Henry Gamadge was endowed by nature with high
spirits and good sense; she therefore reacted cheerfully to
the bright coolness of the following morning—Thursday,
July the second. She put on a dress that was very much
the color of the rambler roses, and looked at herself in the
little glass of the painted bureau, while she arranged the
thick, smooth waves of her hair, with calm determination.

Her hair was brown, her eyes gray, and her mouth
somewhat too wide for the requirements of a Book of
Beauty. Its color, and the color that showed through the
light tan of her cheeks, belonged to youth; she was twenty-
two to Gamadge's thirty-six. This lapse between their ages
did not worry her exactly, but it made her wish to seem
mature in judgment, a companion and a support instead of

a responsibility. She did not like to feel that Gamadge must make allowances for her, especially now that he was burdened with matters more important—she thought—than her own comfort.

She had made up her mind to behave today as Gamadge would have behaved in the same circumstances. She would approach this curious business of the door that opened itself, the watcher in the sunbonnet, Miss Radford's ambiguous behavior about her ownership of the cottage, with a detached and open mind. Clara did not think that she herself was superstitious; she was annoyed with herself for having allowed Maggie to influence her by suggestion. Maggie had certainly done so; without Maggie's conduct and veiled words Clara felt that she might not have given a second thought to the woman in the sunbonnet, or even to the attic door.

After breakfast, therefore, when Miss Radford's old horse and buggy stopped at the bottom of the path, Clara came out to greet her landlady with a bright smile. Miss Radford had a long, yellowish face, a thin, obstinate mouth, a high nose, and a filmy blue eye. She was clothed in what Clara supposed to be half mourning, since—though her black silk dress was sprigged with lavender—she wore black cotton driving gloves and a black chiffon veil; this was looped, with a sad and sombre effect, about the brim of her black straw hat. She looked at Clara through gold-rimmed spectacles.

"Your help says you're having company to supper on the Fourth," she began, in her abrupt way. "I can let you have chickens."

"Oh, thank you, Miss Radford. Yes, the Hunters are driving down."

Miss Radford leaned from her seat to hand Clara a basket which had been on the buggy floor. "Here's the can of milk and the butter. I put in some garden stuff. I can't send Sam over early because I'm shorthanded, like the rest of the folks, and Sam's the only man I've got left."

"It's awfully nice of you to bring things at all." Clara received the basket, and put it down on the grass. "I have my car, you know. I could run over."

"Guess you'd just as soon save your gas and tires for when your husband gets here."

"I would." Clara fondled the nose of the dapple-gray.

"How lucky you are to have this boy and your buggy. It makes you so independent for short trips."

"They come in handy." Miss Radford's eye wandered to indeterminate regions above and behind the cottage. "Is the barn all right for your car? It was roofed last year."

"It's splendid. But if it was good enough for this nice hackney it ought to be good enough for a Ford convertible."

"That's what he is—a hackney. I guess you ride?"

"I used to."

"My sister rode Billy."

"I was so surprised, Miss Radford, when Maggie told me last night that you own the cottage."

"I don't know as it matters. All the business is in the hands of the Hartford agent, and I thought perhaps it wouldn't get out—that I was the owner." Miss Radford's lips curved downward, instead of upward, to show that she was dryly amused. "Try and keep anything from getting out around here!"

"Around anywhere," said Clara.

"I thought perhaps I wouldn't care about the tenants, and it would be just as well if they couldn't come bothering me."

"I'm glad you don't seem to think we will."

"I guess you won't." This seemed to be meant as a compliment, and Clara received it as such. She smiled, looked gratified, and went cheerfully on:

"It was wonderful of you to leave us all that lovely furniture. We'll take good care of it, but I don't know how you could bring yourself to part with it, even for the summer."

"I got some new furniture when I fixed up the farm. I have more than I need right now. You can't hurt that old stuff."

"But it's your family stuff, isn't it?"

"I have lots of family stuff down at the farm. We owned that farm more than a hundred years."

"Oh, did you? And it looks so new," said Clara, who could not bear the way Miss Radford had fixed the farm.

"It was choked with trees, and the doorway rotted. No paint since the last tenants had it."

"I suppose it isn't so easy to get tenants now, for a big farm like that."

"We nearly lost it in 1932. Put a mortgage on; but it's all

clear now. This was our farmer's and dairyman's cottage once."

"It's lovely, the way you had it remodeled. My husband and our friends are going to enjoy it so much. I don't know how you could bear to move away; from the woods, and the waterfall, and everything."

"You try it in winter."

"I'd love to," laughed Clara.

"You couldn't stand it. The only way my sister and I could live here in the cold weather was by shutting off the top floors and blocking the fireplaces and putting up stoves. And half the time the delivery men couldn't get through."

"You and your sister must have slept in those dear little bedrooms downstairs. They're so pretty. And then I suppose you moved upstairs again in the summertime."

"I did; she didn't. She got quite lame."

"The stairs *are* rather steep."

"We put the downstairs bathroom in when she got crippled up with rheumatism. I guess," said Miss Radford, with a glimmer of a smile, "you wouldn't have thought much of the cottage before it was fixed."

"Well, I love it now."

"I was afraid you folks might not like a bathroom opening off the dining room that way, but it had to be there. It was a pantry. Your kitchen wing was built on last fall."

"I think it's very convenient, having the bathroom where it is; but my husband and I will take most of our baths in the pool under the waterfall. I bathe there now."

Miss Radford gazed at her for some moments in a bleak silence. Then she said: "You'll get a cramp; that water's cold as ice."

"Oh, I like it. Did you sleep in the little room with the mysterious door, Miss Radford?"

After a pause Miss Radford said: "I don't know what you mean by a mysterious door."

"The door that doesn't go anywhere. The door without any step, under the lilac bush."

"My sister had that room," said Miss Radford in a cold voice. "When she decided to stay there winters, of course we closed the door up and plugged the keyhole; if she'd lived we would have papered over. I guess you don't know how much wind comes through keyholes and cracks in a cottage like this. The cracks ain't so bad, that door fits quite tight; but if she'd lived we would have papered over."

"I don't suppose you'd want us to have the door opened again for the summer? Mr. and Mrs. Heron's maid will have the room, and it would be nice and cool for her with the door open."

"I guess it had better stay shut. Most people wouldn't care for an outside door to their bedroom, and the new paint will get marred up if we take the plug out and put back the latch."

"Then I'll forget about it," said Clara cheerfully. "Won't you come in, just for a minute, and see how nice everything is?"

"If you'll excuse me, I can't leave old Bill. He don't stand."

"I could get a piece of rope."

"I'd better be getting along home, if you'll excuse me."

"Well, but you must come over and call on me some day; everybody calls on a new neighbor, don't they?"

"I hope you'll excuse me. You'd be surprised how much a farm takes out of you; and that old Sam I have, he can't hardly stoop to dig." Miss Radford picked up the reins and chirped. The gray horse, which had not seemed averse to standing while the conversation went on, slowly extended himself for the pull uphill. The buggy moved away, and up to a slight widening in the road above the cottage.

Clara stood watching her landlady execute the maneuver of the turn; it was accomplished with much chirping on her part, much jerking of first one rein and then the other, much backing and advancing on the part of the gray, and a perilous undercutting of high wheels. As it passed the cottage again Miss Radford bowed stiffly, her hands close together and her wrists high. Clara thought: If Old Bill fell down, he'd drag her over the dashboard.

Maggie came out and took the basket. "Not a wheel did I hear," she said. "This dirt road is as quiet as tanbark."

"She won't come in, Maggie; and I don't think she wants me to go to the farm."

"You'd be ate by the dogs. Nobody can go through that fence of hers unless she comes out and speaks to the animals."

Clara forgot for the moment that she had not intended to discuss these matters with her maid. "I think she hates the cottage. She never once looked at it, and she talks about it as if it were nothing to her."

"Perhaps it's sad for her, on account of the sister dying in it. We ought to be thankful we'll not have her underfoot, counting the broken dishes."

"I wonder whether the sister didn't die in that room with the sealed door."

Maggie's face convinced Clara that that was where the sister had died. Clara walked around the kitchen wing again, pushed aside the sprawling branches of the great lilac, and once more contemplated the yellow panels and the plugged keyhole. The door was blank as a veiled face; it had a strange air of having lost its identity as a door, and become a mere closed chapter in Miss Radford's life.

Clara walked resolutely around to the front of the cottage, along the whole of its length, and up the outside stair to her bedroom. It was the longest route to the attic, but she was not conscious of having followed it for that reason; she would have declared to any listener that it was impossible to be afraid of an attic on a morning like this one.

She went through into the sitting room, and found the hasp tight in its socket; when she levered it up, and swung the flat door towards her, not a breath of air came down from above. Not a breath of air *could* come down, as she discovered when she had climbed the steep flight and emerged into hot dimness; the one low window, which faced to the east, was not only shut; it was sealed with a cobweb. But it was otherwise quite clean, as was the rest of the raftered place; even the floor boards were fairly free of dust—what she could see of them; for the attic, to her surprise, was far from empty. Miss Radford seemed to have left not only a lot of old furniture in the place, but a large trunk. There were some framed pictures, too, standing with their faces against the wall; and there was a big old wardrobe with a drawer under it—a drawer so crammed with books and papers that it could not be entirely closed.

The furniture was horrid stuff, ornate and plush-covered; the pictures shiny chromos, of no possible value; the trunk an old-fashioned monster, initialed *E. R. H.* Its lock hung open. Clara, wondering whether summer tenants were not supposed to need attic room, lifted its lid, and was instantly smothered by an overpowering odor of mothball. Really, this was too bad of Miss Radford; she had left all her winter things in the cottage. Dresses and underclothing; a shawl-like garment; and there in a corner some knitting and a work bag!

Feeling rather disgusted with her landlady, Clara got down on the floor and dragged open the long drawer under the wardrobe. Velvet-bound photograph albums, some old songs in flowery paper covers, old magazines and novels. Clara had never heard of the novels; *The Sorrows of Satan, Chandos, Beauty's Daughters,* but she thought they must surely go back to a day earlier than Miss Radford's own. She pushed the drawer in as far as it would go, got up from the floor, and swung open the doors of the wardrobe.

Here, if you please, was a summer wardrobe! Silk, gingham, voile—straw hats on a shelf. A faded dress and a sunbonnet, purple, with a small black sprig.

These could not be Miss Radford's clothes; none of the things in the attic were Miss Radford's. They were her dead sister's, from the trunk to the furniture, from the sentimental songs and novels to the garments in the wardrobe. Nothing to frighten anybody in that harmless fact, though Miss Radford might have had the common politeness to dispose of the relics before her tenants came in. But that limp purple dress, that sunbonnet hanging by its knotted strings—Clara had seen them, or their phantom replicas, before.

She stood looking at them, or rather she stood looking at nothing, in the pose of one who waits, listens, is afraid to turn. Then at last she pushed the doors to, and went across the attic to the stairs with her back straight, her shoulders rigid, her chin high. She descended, latched the attic door behind her, and walked quickly into and through her own bedroom to the flagstone outside its back door. She sat down on it, breathing hard.

Well; she could write or telephone to the agent and ask to have the things removed; but hadn't she better wait and consult with the Herons before entering upon what might be a controversy? Had she really seen—at some distance—a sunbonnet and a dress like those repulsive-looking things in the wardrobe? Was she getting sunbonnets on the brain?

At least she could get away from them, and from the

cottage, for a while. She had an errand; she must get that man of Mrs. Simms's to look at the latch, and while he was about it he could attend to some doors that stuck. The Herons would not like their bedroom and bathroom doors to stick.

Clara used her car only when she was forced to use it; she liked walking, and now set out on her walk to the Simmses' farm. She went down the little hill behind the cottage, past the windows of the two ground-floor bedrooms, past the kitchen wing and across the field. Most of the Simms property lay on the other side of the highway, next to the Radford land; the farmhouse itself, a small, dingy affair, stood in its unkempt yard not more than a dozen feet from the roadway, backed by a paintless outbuilding or so and a square of vegetable garden. Mrs. Simms, a widow with married children, did not do much farming; she ran her place in a haphazard fashion, keeping it as a sort of rallying place for her clan. Sons, daughters and grandchildren were always staying with her in relays.

The Simmses' dog, a meek setter, escorted Clara to the back door, where fat Mrs. Simms stood waving.

Clara explained that she wanted the services of Web Hawley, the sly-looking thin hired man who lived in the barn. He joined her and his employer as they conversed, and offered himself with some enthusiasm; he had already had experience of Clara's tipping.

Mrs. Simms agreed that he could very well let Mrs. Gamadge have part of his dinner hour.

"Makin' out all right, up there?" she asked.

"Oh, yes; I love it."

"Too bad your friends was kep'. Your help was tellin' me."

"I have so much to do I shan't miss them."

Mrs. Simms laughed for a long time over this naïve remark, and then said she hoped Mis' Gamadge wasn't on foot because there was anything wrong with her car.

"Oh, no; I like walking. I'm going to walk up the Ladder this afternoon to see Mr. and Mrs. Hunter."

"My goodness, Hunters' is a township away!"

"Not if you go by the Ladder."

"That's a walk I wouldn't take for a wager."

"Look out for copperheads," put in Web Hawley. "It's snake weather."

"Don't scare me to death," begged Clara.

Mrs. Simms reminded Web that nobody had seen any copperheads around yet that summer.

"Never knew a summer when one of 'em didn't show up somewheres," insisted Web, who liked to alarm the women.

"I'm real sorry," continued Mrs. Simms, "that I can't help you out with vegetables and milk; but I guess Alvira Radford has plenty to sell. She hasn't got grandchildren to eat her out of provisions."

"Oh, yes; Miss Radford lets me have all I need."

"So your help told me. She's a real nice woman. Walks down here of an evening."

"I understand Miss Radford lost her sister last summer," said Clara. "She must be lonely, I should think."

"Guess so. Mis' Hickson died a year ago this comin' sixth of July, just around sunset, and Alvira had to come and git Web to drive over to Avebury for the doctor. Web had to leave the cows."

"Chased all over Avebury for Doc Knapp," said Web. "Found him at the fair grounds, listenin' to the band. Mis' Hickson was dead, time we got back here."

"Handsome funeral," said Mrs. Simms. "Web helped tote the coffin out."

"Good thing it wasn't winter," said Web. "That cottage is no place for anybody to die in bad weather."

"What did she die of?" asked Clara, with Gamadge and his procedure firmly in mind.

Mrs. Simms looked up at a passing cloud. "Gastric stummick."

Web Hawley added: "Or somethin'," and looked at the cloud too.

"Is Dr. Knapp a good doctor?" asked Clara. "We might need one; you never know."

"He might seem old-fashioned to you folks," said Mrs. Simms.

"I like that kind."

"Well, there's one thing, he's used to the trip. He takes care of us, and he took care of the Radfords for years. Took care of Eva Hickson for this complaint she had, whatever it was, till she died of it. Couple of weeks she was sick, and out he'd come. He'll be comin' out to doctor you, if you walk all day in this heat."

Clara turned to look up at the long range of forest

behind her to the east. She said: "I'm going to follow that
trail in those woods up there and find where it goes."

Mrs. Simms chuckled. "You don't know where you'll
come out?"

"No, where?"

"A cemetery."

Clara, startled, repeated: "A cemetery?"

"Avebury Old Cemetery; the new one's the other side of
town. That trail comes out of the woods just above Avebury,
four five miles below here, and across a field is the old
graveyard."

Clara, after a pause, said that she must take her husband there; he liked old graveyards. She went on in a
casual tone: "By the way, a woman comes along that trail
sometimes, and out on the ridge behind the cottage.
About sundown. I wondered who she was."

"Woman?" Mrs. Simms was puzzled, and Web Hawley
also wrinkled his face up.

"In a sunbonnet. I wondered if she might be helping
you or Miss Radford, or something; so many women are
getting back into farm work on account of the war."

Mrs. Simms turned and looked at her hired man, who
shook his head.

"Quite thin she is," said Clara.

"Then it ain't me," laughed Mrs. Simms. "I never go up
there, anyway, and there's only us and Alvira Radford for
miles. All north of this is the reservation. No women
there!"

"Not in sunbonnets," said Web.

"She doesn't come from my place, and Alvira hasn't any
woman with her except that girl comes in half time; goes
home after dinner. If it's Alvira, it's the first time she ever
did such a thing in her life. When does this woman come,
did you say?"

"About sunset."

"That's suppertime for us folks. Funny," said Mrs. Simms.
But she looked as if she thought summer people might be
capable of mistaking a man or a tree for a woman in a
sunbonnet.

"I thought she might cut through from the route below
here," said Clara. "Then you wouldn't see her."

"There ain't any farmhouse down the route for two
miles."

"Well," said Clara, "it doesn't matter who she is. I only wondered." She stooped to pat the head of the setter. "I do hope," she said, "that this boy doesn't take it into his head to tackle Miss Radford's dogs."

"Real dangerous, those black things," agreed Mrs. Simms, "but she don't let 'em off the place."

"Barred up like a fort," said Web Hawley. "Lucky she bought up the wire for that fence last year; she wouldn't get it now."

"I don't know what she wants of that great fence—or of those dogs, either," objected Clara. "Eli says it's so safe here."

"She's so rich," piped Web Hawley, in a sarcastic voice. "Fellers might hear about it an' come all the way from Hartford or New York."

"Does she keep the money her sister left her in the house?" Clara tried to match her tone with his.

"Nobody knows where she keeps it," said Web. "Her folks don't know, neither, from what I hear."

"I can't see," said Clara, "why if the sister—Mrs. Hickson, did you say her name was?—why if she was so rich they went on living in the cottage, instead of going back to their big house."

"Miser," said Mrs. Simms. "Don't say I said so." She added: "Nobody knew Eva Hickson had money until she was dead and Alvira got it by will."

"Well, I suppose Miss Radford is glad now that she *was* a miser," said Clara. "All the more left for her. I really must be going."

But she had to wait and accept a bunch of outsize pansies; which Mrs. Simms, smiling, did not refuse a quarter for.

Clara went home by the road. Before she turned off the highway, however, she stopped to view Miss Radford's farm with a fresh, if not a pleasurable interest. It was twenty yards beyond the fork, but the two black dogs— Clara thought they must be Doberman pinschers with a hint of Great Dane—would not tolerate the sight of her even at that distance. They rushed to the nearest corner of the six-foot wire fence and barked violently, every tooth bared. Snarled, rather; with long and rasping intakes of breath. Clara tried to ignore them as she looked at the old house. Once, perhaps, it had been pleasant enough, shaded by big trees; but now it was ruined. The trees had been cleared away, all but one great maple, and a cindery-looking gravel path led up to a new, shiny front door. There was a new bay window on the left of this door, and there were plate-glass windows to the right. The house had been painted saffron-yellow.

Depressing. Clara looked beyond at the road which wound uphill and at last vanished among trees. Far up the mountain it met the road that turned right to the Hunters'. Clara, thinking of them, felt better; but a feeling of unreality was growing on her, a sense that the sunny landscape in front of her might dissolve like a transparency in a play, and show her something she had never suspected the existence of behind the familiar and the known. *Things are not what they seem:* a cliché, but might it after all be true?

What was the use of research, if it only led to further doubt and uneasiness? But she would not give it up.

3

Consultation

A small car came into view from the direction of the Radford garage, skirted a driveway which had conveniently been left outside the fence, and approached the highway; Clara, as she turned up the road that led past the cottage, was hailed by its driver in a loud, friendly voice: "You Mrs. Gamadge? You Miss Radford's summer tenant?"

Clara stopped, faced him, and said yes, she was.

He was a spruce young man, red-skinned and round-headed, with a small black mustache. He leaned out of his car window, his straw hat on the back of his head: "Want to ride up to the cottage?"

"No thanks, I need the walk."

"Nothing wrong with your car, I hope? Need gas or tires? I run a garage in Avebury, and I could fix you up." He winked, and then added reassuringly: "Miss Radford's my wife's aunt."

"Thanks very much, I . . ."

The front door of the house opened. Miss Radford appeared first, spoke to the dogs, which stopped barking and began to wag their tails, nodded to Clara, and stood aside. A young woman came out and ran down the steps. When she had reached the gate, and it had snapped shut behind her, Miss Radford withdrew and closed her stout new oaken portal. The young woman paused, raked Clara with a sharp and none too amiable look, and then glanced haughtily at the driver of the car.

"Here's my wife, Mrs. Gamadge," he shouted. "Introduce you."

The young woman advanced, now smiling. Clara had an impression first of bright color, then of hollow pink cheeks, large protruding eyes, a thin red mouth, and a mass of yellow hair under a red hat.

"I'm Mrs. Groby," she said. "Miss Radford's niece."

"How do you do?" Clara shook hands. Mrs. Groby's dress was red and white, her bracelets red, her bag and sandals of the most vivid scarlet. She, also, had a loud, high voice.

"Aunt Alvira was telling me your friends couldn't come for two weeks," she went on, her eyes passing rapidly from Clara's hair to her sport shoes, and back again.

"No, but—"

"It's a crime. You must be lonesome."

"No, I like the cottage so much."

"I haven't seen it since it was fixed. We live in Avebury, and we don't get out here very often, but anything we can do, you let us know. It must be terrible for you with no electricity. Hope you get ice?"

"Yes, every day. It's perfect, thank you."

"Aunt Alvira is a kind of a recluse, but she wants you to be comfortable."

"Everything's fine."

Mr. Groby, at first somewhat quelled by the presence of his wife, now recovered his raffish air. He again leaned out of the car, a white oblong in his hand. "Have my card," he urged. "In case of what I said. Fuel and equipment."

Mrs. Groby snatched the card from his hand. "We ain't looking for business," she said angrily, "this is social. I hope you'll drop in when you're down our way, Mrs. Gamadge; any time."

"You must come and see me," said Clara, "but I hope you'll telephone first, because I'm out practically all day."

"You wouldn't care for us to stop in now, just to see how you're fixed?"

"I'd love it, but I have a man doing some work."

"I'll be over some other day."

Mrs. Groby climbed into the car, her husband turned it, and they drove off. Clara went up to the cottage, where Hawley was already at work on the doors.

"There ain't a thing the matter with that latch your help showed me," he said. "Just shove the tongue in good, and it'll stay. All these doors is warped, warped half off their hinges. I seen Groby hail you; did he try to sell you on his black market?"

"I don't really know what you mean, Web."

Mr. Hawley accepted this mild rebuke in good part, and went on planing. Clara had a bathe in the pool, wrote letters, and had lunch. After lunch she busied herself about the cottage until it was time to take her walking stick and start her climb up the Ladder to Mountain Ridge Farm.

The Ladder trail was a steep and winding track, washed into ruts and mudholes by the spring rains. The stream that fed the waterfall and pool ran beside it on the right, then on the left; Clara had to be careful in crossing the old log bridge, hardly more than a trestle now. The Ladder smelled of last year's leaves, this year's mint and pine, damp earth and running water. Halfway up, in a kind of little clearing, there was a flat rock beside the trail; Clara liked to sit here and have a cigarette before she went on—past the tall grass and crumbling foundations of a vanished farm—to more open country, whence she could see the Hunters' ridge in the distance.

There was a well-kept road along the ridge, where Hunters had owned property for a hundred and eighty years, and farmed it until the end of the other war; but the present Phineas Hunter, like Mrs. Simms, had given up farming for profit. He had always used Mountain Ridge Farm as a country place, but had not often come there until 1939; after that he and his wife had spent at least a month in the old house every summer. This year they had come up from New York in June, and proposed to stay until October.

The long, low farmhouse had been cleverly remodeled many years before, its front left intact, its new rooms built out to the edge of the mountain, with a view across vast reaches of treetops to the blue of a Berkshire range and the pale tracery of further ranges beyond. Within doors it had been made comfortable, even luxurious, without being spoiled; it was now the Hunters' second home.

Clara walked along the ridge road, her eyes on the view, until she passed the Hunter barns and outbuildings on the right, and approached the flagged path on the left. She went up to a white doorway, and plied a knocker that had been polished to a soft brightness more like gold than brass. There was no bell; Hunter said that he liked to hear a knocking at the door.

Fanny Hunter came to the door herself. Slim, beautiful, with the complexion and bright, soft hair of a child, she looked no older than her guest. She was in fact thirty, but she had the kind of blondness that does not fade. At the end of her life her hair would be brilliant silver instead of brilliant gold.

She threw up her arms. "Clara—Alonzo has gone to the war!"

"Oh dear, how hard."

"Of course we'll manage, and Phin is such an angel, he never complains. But it is so funny to have fat old Annie, our farmer's wife, you know, bringing in tea and waiting at table. There simply aren't any young women to be had."

"I know."

Mrs. Hunter took Clara's arm. "Are you tired? It's such a climb."

"I'm not a bit tired."

"Then let's go in and see Phin; he's pining for you."

They went along the hall to Hunter's study at the back of the house. It had a screened porch overhanging the wooded mountainside, but today he was working indoors, beside his north window. The study, designed by himself, was ceiled and paneled in native woods, with carvings of oak leaves, acorns and pine cones. The curtains and upholstery were in green silk, and engravings of eighteenth-century personages hung on the rough-plastered walls. Hunter was something of an authority on that period, but in his writing he kept to its byways; he said he had not the learning to approach the great shrines by the traveled roads.

Gamadge's own writing had long since brought him into Hunter's orbit, a little matter of a disputed letter from—as Hunter put it—one of Pope's dunces to another; the two had met at long intervals, then Gamadge had dined with the Hunters, and after he married the two couples had dined together at least once a year. Clara was a great favorite with both the Hunters. She had until now looked upon them as delightful but casual friends; but in the week since her arrival at the cottage she had come to feel as if she had known them intimately all her life.

Now, as Hunter rose from behind his big working-table, she thought again that he was one of the most charming men she had ever met in her life. He was in his middle forties, dark-haired and with dark blue eyes; always rather tanned from outdoor sports—he rode, swam, sailed, golfed, and played a certain amount of tennis—he had not only escaped a scholar's stoop, but had preserved a naturally good figure and an excellent digestion. His best feature was his mouth, a fine bow which seemed always to curve upward; perhaps because he had had the good fortune to be able to make his hobby his profession. Certainly it alone would never have supported him and his wife, or even have fed them in the style to which they were accustomed. Fanny, whom he adored, was just the wife for him; he did not much care for literary society, and valued Gamadge for the latter's companionable quality.

"Well, my dear child," he said, coming around the table, "what do you hear from your good husband?"

"He may be coming home soon, Mr. Hunter."

"Good. Whatever he's doing, it must be pretty thrilling, by Jove. They're going to fit me in somewhere next fall, they tell me, and I hope they'll give me something more exciting than draft board, and less exciting than air wardenship; both of which jobs I shall be glad to exchange for one demanding mental activity. But I confess that I shall miss my nice white hat."

Fanny said: "He's patient, poor darling, about not having a good library to sit in any more."

"My dear, I have many good libraries to sit in, though I do prefer the Bodleian. The trouble is that when I'm at the farm I cannot decently work trips to large libraries into the war effort. Just now I'm stuck for a reference. I wish Gamadge were here; I'm sure he knows all about Pope."

"I don't think he does," said Clara. "He always says that Pope is a great romantic poet, but I know that at school they said that was wrong."

Hunter declared that Pope was a great romantic poet, and everything else great besides. "Are we having tea here, Fanny, or in the other room?"

"I think the other room will be easier for Mrs. Colley."

Hunter, with a low groan, followed his wife and Clara into the yellow drawing room which ran from the study to the front of the house. It was long and low, and had been beautifully done up with yellow satin and brocade. There was an old French landscape over the mantel, and an old French carpet covered the floor. "To the devil with kitchen furniture in the parlor," Hunter was wont to say. "This house is our 'seat,' and it's tight as a drum. The Chippendale fares better here than it would in the steam heat in town."

"But we shall need steam heat or something here, darling," objected Fanny, "if we stay so long."

Hunter patted her shoulder. "We shall contrive something."

"Well, I'm glad we are staying. So many people are, this year, and they let me work in the Stratfield hospital without taking any nursing courses."

"My dearest child," said Hunter, "one does not need training of any kind in order to carry cocoa and lemonade to sick persons. You are more qualified to do that than Mrs. Colley is, I believe."

Fanny shushed him as Mrs. Colley, the farmer's wife, staggered in with the great silver tea tray. She then brought a tray of bread-and-butter and cakes, and retired to a chorus of thanks from her employers.

"And yet, do you know, Clara," said Hunter, while Fanny poured the tea, "it's really very restful, the sense that one must now stay put. All our lives we have been waiting to do the next thing; now we must think twice before we demand our trunks and bags. Are you going to be happy, alone in your cottage until Dick and his wife turn up?"

"Oh, yes. I'm sketching, you know, the most awful daubs, but I love to."

"You have only to say the word, one word; Fanny has your room ready for you, and Maggie will be a blessing to us as things go."

"I certainly shan't settle down on you with Alonzo gone!"

"*I* couldn't stay there alone," said Fanny, handing her her tea.

"My dear, that corner of the world is as safe a corner as there is today, and as lovely a one," said Hunter.

"You and Fanny being here make it right for me," said Clara. "You're surely coming to dinner with me on Saturday night? You won't mind missing the Avebury fireworks and town band?"

"Of course we're coming."

"There's a disappointment, though; Gil Craye can't be with us. We won't get any bridge."

Hunter took his cup of tea from his wife, and settled himself more deeply in his chair. "I regret the bridge," he said, his mouth curving up at one corner, "but I shall survive the absence of Gilbert Craye. He has been what I can only describe as underfoot this summer."

Fanny said: "He's lonely. It must be awful not to be able to use one's eyes."

"Well, my dear, he uses his freely—except for purposes that I really think are not essential to his happiness. He can play bridge."

"Poor Gil, he adores you; don't be mean about him."

Hunter said gently: "I don't wish to be mean about him; and if he presumes a little on his disability, I don't much blame him; but I can't help hoping that Clara is prepared to take him more or less off our hands. Do you like our poor little rich boy, Clara?"

Clara replied that she and Gamadge were rather fond of Gil Craye, but that they didn't see much of him in town, and she had thought Stratfield too far for them to see much of him here.

"I must confess," said Hunter, "that I sometimes wish Stratfield were farther. You know, I'm afraid that if Pope had known him, Pope would have taken his pen in hand and produced something memorable." Hunter joined his finger tips, closed his eyes, and murmured:

> "*Flits in the sunlight, mindless as a fly,*
> *And knows no bliss that money cannot buy.*"

Then, opening his eyes and smiling at the ceiling, he murmured: "Something of that kind, perhaps."

"Oh dear," said Fanny, laughing, "is that Pope?"

"Pope? Great Heavens, no! Only me," said Hunter, "and a feeble imitation too; and quite unfair to our friend. But satirical couplets don't succeed by being generous."

"I'm glad you admit it's unfair!" Fanny shook her head at him.

"Unfair, but only because so little bliss of any kind can be obtained in this imperfect world without money. Mine can't, yours can't, Clara's can't. Gamadge's couldn't—it cost money, Clara, to produce someone whom Gamadge could love."

"He talks like that," complained Fanny with a pathetic look at Clara, "and mixes me all up."

"I don't intend to mix you up, my dearest," said Hunter. "I thought I was clarifying the matter."

"Henry clarifies things for me, too," said Clara, "and mixes me up frightfully." She was trying to think of some way to gain reassurance from her friends without making too much of the situation at the cottage. She plunged: "I hear that Miss Radford—at the farm, you know—owns our cottage. I was so surprised."

"Surprised?" Hunter raised an eyebrow. "I could have told you that; in fact, I believe I did mention it to Dick Heron. Or didn't I? I dare say I only gave him the name of the agent. Why should you be surprised?"

"Well, it's so pretty and so nicely done over, and I've been buying eggs of her. I thought she was just a farm woman."

"She is an ordinary farm woman," said Hunter, "but she came into money." He glanced at his wife, who looked rather uncomfortable, Clara thought, and went on: "She probably took advice about the cottage, since she wanted to rent it to summer people; but she did the farm over to suit herself."

"She must be a disagreeable old thing," said Fanny. "They told me at the hospital that it wasn't any use to ask her for a contribution, though she's so rich, because she always says she only gives through her church organization."

"Well, my dear," said Hunter, "these magnates must stick to their budgets or they'd be swamped. You must remember, besides, that it's the first time any Radford—except the sister who married the button man—has had any cash to spend. They've had that farm," he told Clara, "almost as long as we've had this one."

"I think her money must have made her a little crazy," said Clara. "She's put that great fence up, and she has those awful dogs."

"She's probably in the processs of becoming a real old-fashioned New England recluse," said Hunter, while Fanny again glanced nervously at him and away. "Our farmer, who keeps us informed of local gossip—if you can call it local—tells me that she hasn't set foot in her church since the sister died. Gives to those organizations, you know, but won't go to meeting. The minister, I believe, has wrestled with her in vain. Hang it all, even I have to go once in a summer; it's expected of us. My father dragged us all into the family pew every month, and my grandfather sat there twice every Sunday."

"Mrs. Groby says she's a recluse already," said Clara.

"Oh, you've met the Grobys?" Hunter smiled.

"Horrid, horrid little man," exclaimed Fanny. "I hate to stop for gas at his filling station."

"But I understand that he's most accommodating," said Hunter, "if people run out of gas or wear out a tire."

"He said something to me," admitted Clara.

"How does he dare?" wondered Fanny.

"My dear," said her husband, "I'm sure that there was no witness to the conversation; there never is. Don't waste horror on Groby; his type will always bootleg something or other, and think it commendable business enterprise."

"Mrs. Groby is coming to call on me," said Clara.

Fanny moaned, and Hunter laughed. "Of course she'll call," he said. "She's called on Fanny. She drove all the way up from Avebury once, a good ten miles, to solicit a contribution to *her* war fund."

"I wasn't in," said Fanny, "thank goodness."

"I was." Hunter, lighting Clara's cigarette and his own, smiled at the memory. "I thought her vain and strident, but oddly sensitive in her own way. I knew her history. The only Radford son, Alvira's brother, was a traveling salesman, and he married a waitress somewhere in the West. Mrs. Groby was the sole result of the union."

"Now I understand her better," said Clara. "I thought she was a funny kind of niece for Miss Radford to have."

"I understand that Alvira doesn't see the joke; Colley says she doesn't care for the Grobys at all."

"They were calling on her this morning, though."

"Of course they were; Alvira inherited one hundred thousand dollars, if rumor can be believed."

"A hundred and six thousand," said Clara, while the Hunters laughed. "Mrs. Simms and her hired man told us. Can she possibly be keeping it in the house? Can that be why she has the fence and the dogs?"

The Hunters said nothing. Clara, after an irresolute look at their faces, went hastily on:

"I know you know something about Miss Radford, and about that money, and about the sister's death. I know there's something queer about it. Mrs. Simms knows what it is, and Web Hawley knows, and I'm sure Mrs. Simms has told Maggie. I wish you'd tell me; I don't mind a bit about the sister dying in the cottage, it can't be that; there's something more."

There was a pause, during which Fanny looked distressed and Hunter thoughtful. At last he said: "She'll get it from somebody else, Fanny."

"Oh, Phin, but it can't be true; why repeat it?"

"Well, it was through us that Dick Heron heard about the cottage."

"Because he was inquiring about a place here for themselves and the Gamadges. It isn't our fault. Clara, we never heard a word of it until after Dick had signed the lease, and it's all nonsense, and we hoped you'd never hear of it either. Mrs. Hickson died of something that happened to her after she had intestinal flu, and Dr. Knapp, who's perfectly reliable, signed the certificate. He wouldn't have done that if there had been the slightest question. It's all just country spite."

Clara put out her cigarette. "They're saying that Miss Radford poisoned her sister for the money?"

Hunter, after a troubled look at her, spoke gently: "The thing seemed to me too farcical a notion to bother Dick Heron with; if I had thought there was a grain of truth in it I should have written to him. As Fanny suggests, it was very trying for the neighbors—Alvira's sudden acquisition of wealth; I don't think the Radford sisters were too popular. I believe they were considered a trifle close-fisted, even in a community of traditional cheeseparers. But even if the thing were a fact, Clara, Alvira Radford wouldn't poison you, you know. You're a source of income.

However, perhaps you'd better, after all, come up to us; Gamadge might prefer it."

Clara asked: "Is she afraid they'll mob her, or something? Is that why she put up the fence and got the dogs?"

"I'm not at all sure that she's ever heard the gossip, or ever will before it dies out of its own ineptitude. She's bought herself a few sticks of new furniture, perhaps, or put in new piping; she probably overvalues her possessions. She's dizzy with her hundred and six thousand."

"If she has heard the story, and didn't poison Mrs. Hickson, all she would have to do would be to dig Mrs. Hickson up."

Hunter burst into uncontrollable laughter; Fanny cried: "What a ghastly idea! Clara, how can you?"

Hunter was, after another paroxysm, able to address his wife: "You forget, Fanny; Clara is married to Henry Gamadge. She sups on horrors; she takes an exhumation in her stride."

Clara said stolidly: "If she's so eccentric that she put up the fence just to protect plumbing and chairs, she may be eccentric enough to come and stare at the cottage."

"Stare at the cottage?" Fanny stared too—at Clara.

"Some woman in a sunbonnet comes out of the woods behind us and stands and looks at the cottage."

"Well, but, Clara, couldn't it be just anybody? Country people are so curious about us."

"I don't know who she could be, and that trail she comes and goes by doesn't end anywhere; except," added Clara lightly, "at the Avebury cemetery."

"Good Heavens," said Hunter. "We seem to be getting very funereal. How often has this woman in a sunbonnet come and looked at the premises, Clara?"

"Three times; last Thursday—the day after I came, and Sunday, and yesterday."

"At three-day intervals; she seems to be on a schedule," said Hunter. "Unless she's come at other times, and you've missed her."

"She always seems to come at sunset."

"Dear me." Hunter considered, his eyes vague. "Alvira may be turning into a 'case,' one can't tell; but I should have said that curious or not, she'd be mortally afraid of intruding; just as she, and all her type, are mortally afraid of being intruded upon."

"I don't think it *is* Miss Radford, somehow. She doesn't seem like Miss Radford. The sunbonnet hides her face, but I don't think Maggie thinks it's Miss Radford, either. Maggie's seen her, too."

Fanny said that Clara ought to speak to the state police.

"It would seem so silly—just on account of a woman in a sunbonnet."

"And that trail is probably a right of way. Still," said Hunter, "I might mention the thing to Eli, or old Duckett at Avebury."

"I'll let you know if she comes again."

How, Clara wondered as she rose to go, could she ever explain to these friends, to anybody but Gamadge, that the matter was perhaps to be looked at from a different point of view? She couldn't face the look that would come into Fanny's eyes, into Hunter's eyes, if she began to argue the question of the attic door and the attic itself. She couldn't ask them to consider whether the woman in the sunbonnet mightn't have been dead a year.

4

No Flowers

The walk home down the Ladder was invigorating; more invigorating was her encounter with Eli the Indian, who took it entirely for granted that she would stay on with Maggie until the others came. He did not think it wonderful that two women should live alone in a cottage, within sight of other houses, and with a telephone on the premises. Miss Radford had lived there entirely alone for years, until her sister came back after the button man died.

Maggie greeted her cheerfully from the porch, there was a smell of baking, the waterfall splashed and hummed. This was what she had promised Gamadge—his own place, not a visit in a formal house. This was what he was looking forward to.

She got out her sketching things, and prepared them for work tomorrow; she meant to paint the sycamore below the cottage—if she could. Then she had a bath in the pool, and a large supper. She went to bed early and slept well.

Friday was a day of furious preparation, since Maggie had her own ideas about a style of entertainment suitable for the Hunters. Flowers must be everywhere, the blue downstairs bedroom must be arranged as a powder room for Mrs. Hunter, the green bedroom next it adapted to Mr. Hunter's requirements, if he had any. The turquoise bathroom must be fitted out with all Clara's best assortment of towels, toilet waters and soap; they were unfortunately pink, and did not match the bathroom; but fortunately they matched one another.

Clara was sent out early in the car to see whether Miss Radford had flowers. She drove to the farm, blew her horn, and allowed Miss Radford to come to the gate. She had no wish to be escorted to the front door by two dogs, sniffing at her ankles as she had seen them sniff at Mrs. Groby's.

"I don't get a minute to grow flowers," said Miss Radford. "When I need flowers I get them in the field. It's full of black-eyed Susans now."

"I'll just drive in to Avebury, then, Miss Radford. There's a nice-looking nursery there."

"Seems a pity to buy flowers, with all those ramblers on your porch."

"The Hunters are coming to dinner tomorrow, and I thought I'd like a variety—something for the table."

"Seems a pity. I'm going to get some black-eyed Susans tomorrow, and some ferns—for the cemetery. I might bring you some, if you haven't time to pick."

"Or why shouldn't I get you some, when I get mine? I'd love to give you a bunch for the cemetery, nice big ones, gladiolus perhaps, or stock." Clara thought: Sunday is the day they put flowers on graves. It's Mrs. Hickson's anniversary—at least Monday is, but Miss Radford would decorate the grave on Sunday. She wouldn't dare to, if . . . Or would she have to, on account of the neighbors?

Miss Radford was politely refusing Clara's proposed gift, on the ground that the other things lasted longer. "I'll just go up to the woods along your road and take a pail. Ferns there—they last a month in a pail."

Clara drove to the nursery in Avebury, and ordered a dazzling assortment, principally of sweet peas, to be cut and delivered the next morning. When she reached the cottage again she hastily collected her sketching things and went down the road to a point below the sycamore, but a melodious honking brought her back around the bend. A magnificent car, low and shiny as a motor launch, stood humming at the foot of the path; Mr. Gilbert Craye sat in it among gadgets like semi-precious stones, the sun glinting on his thick-lensed spectacles.

He was a study in brown; his checked suit being an almost perfect match in both its tones for his thin, freckled face and his sun-bleached hair. He was always laughing, which perhaps accounted for the deep wrinkles around his eyes and from his nostrils to his chin: certainly they did not come from age—he was barely thirty. He was fragile-looking but wiry, always meticulously groomed, and oddly placative—a man, one would have said, unsure of his welcome.

It is true that he had had to outlive a certain reputation. A neglected child, a wild boy, he had married ridiculously and very young. There had been disagreeable publicity over his divorce, over the death of his only child, a boy; it had died in infancy, at his house at Stratfield, while he was away somewhere. The divorced wife had made a frightful row. For the last half-dozen years he had lived alone—except for a stream of supposedly unpresentable friends—in his old house at Stratfield, in Florida or on his California ranch; but just of late he was supposed to have quieted down, and people were inviting him to dinner again.

Gamadge had known his family, called him by his first name, and had never ceased to see him occasionally in New York. Craye was plainly an admirer of Clara's, but always treated and addressed her with formality—as though he wished the Gamadges to know that he could behave correctly when he chose.

He now said, smiling as usual from ear to ear, "I'm terribly sorry about tomorrow night, Mrs. Gamadge; brought you a couple of peace offerings." He got out as Clara approached, and extricated two large market baskets from the rumble.

"Oh, Gil, it's too much!" Clara gazed in rapture at

garden lettuce, a duck, a pound of butter, a jar of thick cream, and an assortment of vegetables.

"I know what the markets in Avebury are like, and the farmers separate the milk almost before it's out of the cow. Thought you might want to make ice cream, or something."

"Maggie! Maggie! See what Mr. Craye brought us."

Maggie came out, all smiles for Craye, and refused help with the baskets. While she lugged them into the dining room he continued to rummage in the car, lifted his head at last, and gazed at Clara in consternation. "Damn. I forgot the flowers."

"I've ordered flowers."

"I'll go back."

"You'll do no such thing. I've ordered flowers in Avebury. Gil, you really are an angel; the trout on Wednesday, and now all those lovely things."

"They're all off the place; I caught the trout myself. I hope Gamadge will want to help me fish my stream."

"He will, and so will I."

"You're going to ask me over again, aren't you?"

"Of course. When the Herons get here we'll have lots of bridge."

"How's Mrs. Hunter? I thought she was looking tired the other day when she was in Stratfield; too much hospital work."

"She's all right. Alonzo's gone."

"Oh, Lord. I'm cutting down on the gardens myself, like everybody else. You know you haven't been over to look at the old place yet. How about now? Jump in; stay to lunch."

"I can't today, Gil, thank you."

"It's not much of a run if we take the reservation road; worth a few bumps to cut off the extra miles."

"I really mustn't, today."

His light eyes observed her keenly through his glasses. He said: "It's perfectly O.K., you know. All the dowagers come, and matrons of all ages. They drop in to lunch whenever they feel like it."

"Of course. I'll do it soon."

He got back into his car, and sat surveying the yellow front of the cottage. "Very nice," he said. "Old Alvira had them do a good job on it. It used to be a forbidding kind of little witch's den. How do you like her?"

"Miss Radford? I like her well enough."

If Craye were really one of the ephemera, he was at least not dull-witted. He heard the uncertainty in Clara's voice, and looked at her sharply. "Any reason for not liking her?" he asked.

"Oh dear; I suppose that story has got as far as Stratfield."

"My dear girl," said Craye, but he did not look at her now; he turned his head and stared at the trees that hid the stream. "My dear Mrs. Gamadge, the old creature has friends in Stratfield—charming women. Sewing and snooping done cheap."

"Well, I think it's dreadful that they should spread such a story about her, just because she came into money."

"Story about *her*? What are we talking about?" Craye looked quickly around at Clara again.

"I thought we were talking about people saying that poor Miss Radford poisoned her sister for her money."

Craye gazed at her for a moment with his mouth open, and then burst out laughing. "Do they really say that? I'm tickled to death!"

"Why? And what were *you* talking about before?"

"Nothing. Forget it." He slowly backed the long car until it reached the widening in the road; then, facing her, he asked: "Seen your friend Schenck lately?"

"Not very lately. He's out of town so much since he's been with the F.B.I. He's so happy—it was his dream."

"I imagine he and Gamadge must have some wonderful powwows about secret missions and stuff?"

"I don't think they tell each other anything, and they certainly don't tell me!"

Craye, laughing, said that no doubt it was all very hush-hush, turned the car, and drove rather slowly away. He always drove carefully; he could not afford to jeopardize his license. He had never had an accident in his life.

The rest of the day passed pleasantly, Clara spending most of it getting purple patches into her study of the sycamore. She had another uneventful evening and night, and woke on Saturday morning feeling very cheerful. There was no malignant influence in this charming place, she had been completely mistaken to think so. She had simply allowed herself to build up a series of unrelated facts into a morbid whole. Maggie had unlatched the attic door and forgotten it; the dress and sunbonnet in the

wardrobe upstairs were nothing like the dress and sunbonnet worn by the harmless stroller on the ridge; or if they
were, why should they not be? There were probably not
so many patterns of cotton print to be had in Avebury.
Perhaps it was rather startling, after all the rest of the
happenings, to learn that Miss Radford was being accused
of doing away with her sister; but Phineas Hunter said she
hadn't done away with her sister, and in that case none of
the rest of it meant anything. Certainly Clara was not
going to let morbid fancies spoil this paradise for her.

In the afternoon she arranged her flowers. She had filled
the last vase, and was gathering up string and scissors
from the porch, when the sun began to sink behind the
topmost branches of the trees across the road. The Hunters would be along soon; they liked plenty of time for
cocktails, and a late dinner. "Dinner, thank God," said
Hunter, "is not a picnic. It requires artificial light."

Miss Radford's antiquated rig came slowly down the
road. She sat erect as usual under the hood of the buggy,
ferns and black-eyed Susans massed about her feet; the
gray horse plodded along demurely, as if conscious that he
must not allow a drop of water to spill out of the pails.

He approached, Miss Radford gave her tenant a stiff
bow, and Clara bowed in return. She was about to say
something about the vegetation in the buggy, had indeed
opened her mouth to say it, and then everything seemed
to happen at once; in what order, Clara was never afterwards able to remember. But the whole thing was over in
thirty seconds; the old horse had checked, swerved, and
reared, his feet pawing the air; the buggy was going over, a
shaft broke with a noise like a pistol shot, the gray went
down with it. He was lashing out, entangled in his reins,
as Clara, with one blinding look over her shoulder to see
what had frightened him, dashed down the path.

The look was enough. It stood at the corner of the
house, gaunt and menacing; a flat brownness showing
between the limp sides of the sunbonnet, a hand, brown
and shrivelled as a withered leaf, at the end of an outstretched
arm. Its skirt or apron was flapping; it might have been a
scarecrow, blowing in the wind.

It was there, it was gone. Clara had no time for it, not
now; Miss Radford was somewhere in the wreckage of the
buggy, perhaps within reach of the gray's heels. He was

kicking wildly, as Clara rounded him and began to drag
Miss Radford out from under a cascade of yellow daisies,
ferns and water. Maggie appeared, and without a word
took over. Clara loosened traces, tore at buckles, and had
old Bill on his feet. He stood docile. She led him free of
the broken shaft, and he walked mildly away from her up
the yard.

Clara ran back to the recumbent figure in the road.
Maggie had dipped a corner of her apron in the water
remaining in one of the pails, and was bathing Miss
Radford's face; it was bleeding.

"Is she dead, Maggie?" Clara was panting as if she had
run a mile.

"Dead? Why would a fall like that kill her? I don't know
that she's even hurt. She's fainted from the shock."

"Her cheek is bleeding."

"Just a bit of a scratch. Wait, now, is her foot right?"

Clara, her teeth chattering, inspected a black, laced
shoe. It lay flat on the road. "I think her ankle must be
broken."

"We'll get her into the house and call the doctor. Get
one of the straw mats off the porch, ma'am, and slip it
under her legs."

"Ought we to move her, Maggie?"

"We can't leave her here in the dust, and her bleeding.
We'll put her on the green bed—it's all made and ready."

Clara got one of the small stiff mats from the porch, and
slid it under Miss Radford's legs. It was easy to lift her,
easy to carry her up the path. Old Bill, who had been
peacefully cropping long grass, lifted his head to watch
them go by. He had detached himself, he would forever-
more remain detached from the accident.

"What in wonder scared the beast?" asked Maggie. "Or
was she trying to turn short, or what?"

"Didn't you—didn't you see it?"

"Not a thing did I see, till I heard you screaming and
crying for me."

"I didn't even know I called you."

"Indeed you did, and I ran out, and you were dragging
the old lady out of the ferns and water, and the horse with
his foot through the dashboard."

Maggie backed against the screen of the dining-room

doorway; Miss Radford's filmy eyes opened, and she began to struggle.

"It's all right, ma'am," said Maggie.

"No! No!"

Clara said: "Maggie, she doesn't want to go in the cottage."

But Maggie went on backing, and Clara had to follow or drop her share of the burden. They entered the dining room, and Maggie resolutely backed on. "She's not herself, ma'am." And indeed Miss Radford seemed to have fainted again.

"She's fainted again, Maggie."

"Why wouldn't she, with the pain of her ankle?"

"Not in that bedroom, Maggie. The other one."

"The first one is the right one, and I wouldn't have her on the blue spread for anything, with the blood trickling down."

As they entered the little green room with the door that went nowhere, Clara thought: It's just like a nightmare. I can't do anything. The horse saw it, and so did Miss Radford. I mustn't leave her alone. I'll make Maggie stay with her while I telephone.

Miss Radford was laid on the bed, and Maggie got dry clothes for her, towels and cold water. When she returned, Clara went and called up Dr. Knapp at Avebury.

He answered in person. "I'll be right out, Mrs. Gamadge. Did she hit her head, do you know?"

"My maid says there doesn't seem to be any sign of it, Doctor."

"Don't move her again till I come. You think her ankle's broken?"

"Yes."

"Too bad. Too bad. Give her a pillow, and don't do another thing till I get there. I'm glad you have somebody to help you. We're short of nurses, you know."

"I know. I've done a little hospital work, and my maid is splendid."

"I couldn't get one out there tonight for love or money, but tomorrow I'll have an ambulance there if I have to drive it myself."

"She—she came to for a second, Doctor; she doesn't want to be here."

There was a short pause, and then the doctor's reassuring bass came over the wire again: "She'll have to stay tonight. She ought to be glad you're willing to look after her. I'll bring what I have on hand, but I'll want a prescription filled later. Have you anybody to send to Avebury?"

"Mr. and Mrs. Hunter are coming."

"Good; Hunter will drive in for me. I'll be with you in fifteen minutes."

Clara went back to the bedroom. Miss Radford lay under a blanket, her eyes open, and her face set in an expression of grim endurance.

"It's all right, Miss Radford," said Clara. "Doctor Knapp is on the way."

Miss Radford's voice was the stronger of the two: "I don't know what got into me to let such a thing happen; I don't know what got into Billy," she said. "I don't mean to stay here and impose on you. Knapp will have to get me home."

"We'll take good care of you till they can send an ambulance."

"I can't be sick in somebody else's house. Knapp will have to get me home tonight."

"It's your own cottage." Clara met the pale-blue eyes; in them she read amazement, and the determination to conceal it as far as it could be concealed by mortal effort. "Don't worry, Miss Radford," she went on. "We won't leave you a minute. You'll be right with us, and the Hunters are coming."

"Where's Billy?"

"Out in the yard, mowing the grass. I'm going out to water him and cover him up till your man gets here."

Miss Radford closed her eyes. Clara waited until Maggie came back into the room, and then got a piece of clothesline and a bucket of water. She went out, tied the gray to a tree, got his harness off, and gave him a drink. Then she went up to get a rug from the second-floor sitting room. The attic door was wide open, but she did not even wait to close it; it was only another horror among horrors, and her bewildered mind refused to deal with it.

She took the rug from the sofa, and went down and into the yard. As she covered the old horse, straightening the blanket with precision, the Hunters drove up in their open car. They looked very festive, and it was rather funny to see their faces change as they caught sight of the fallen-buggy, the broken shaft, and the heap of ferns and flowers.

"Ye heavenly powers," said Hunter, transfixed, "what's this?"

"There's been an accident," shrieked Fanny. "Clara, is that Miss Radford's rig? What's happened to Miss Radford?"

"She's hurt her foot," said Clara. "The doctor's coming. I'm so sorry about dinner."

"Dinner!" Phineas Hunter helped his wife out of the car, and then came up to Clara and took hold of her arm above the elbow. "You need a doctor yourself. You look very green, Clara; where's your whiskey?"

5

Twenty Minutes to One

The Hunters were magnificent. They refused to be guests, they took entire charge of the cottage, they would not even consider going home that night. Fanny sat with Miss Radford—who, after one startled look at her radiant nurse's flowered dinner dress and multicolored earrings, shut her eyes and remained in a kind of obstinate trance—while Maggie rescued the dinner from the stove and set a table in the sitting room upstairs. That was Hunter's idea, and he helped place and lay it. Clara, passing through, saw that the attic door had been closed. He detained her.

"Come and sit down a minute, Clara, until Knapp gets here, and tell me how the thing happened."

Clara felt much better; the arrival of the Hunters had changed the whole aspect of things. She had had a stiff drink of whiskey, and Miss Radford's condition pushed less material anxieties into the background. She found herself able to talk without difficulty, and she was glad to sit down beside Hunter and tell him part of the tale:

"It was that woman in the sunbonnet. She came around the house and frightened the horse."

"Woman in a sunbonnet?" Hunter looked at her, frowning. "You know, the one I told you about on Thursday."

"The one who's been prowling around back of the cottage?"

"Yes. I think her apron had been flapping. I only saw her for a second, but I think she backed off around the corner of the cottage. I was running to get Miss Radford away from the horse's heels."

"Well, upon my word, this is a little too much! I'll certainly speak to the state police tomorrow. This can't go on—it's more than an annoyance, it's positively a menace. I suppose you didn't have a chance afterwards to go after her? You or Maggie?"

"Maggie didn't see her at all, this time. I was rather worried later; I was afraid she might still be on the premises somewhere." Clara glanced at the attic door. Hunter, seeing the look, rose.

"I'll soon settle that!"

"Oh—thank you."

He went up into the attic, came back again, and made a search of the cottage, indoors and out. He even went to the old barn where Clara kept the car. When he came back he shook his head. "Not anywhere."

"I almost think she isn't real."

"Isn't real?"

No, thought Clara, I can't say it; I simply can't. But she went on: "There's something so queer about her."

"We'll soon find out whether she's real or not! She may be a half-wit, camping in the woods; perhaps I'd better call up the barracks at Stratfield tonight."

"Oh, no; you're here."

"I certainly am, and now Knapp's here—that's his car."

The doctor, a short, stoutish man of sixty with a clipped gray beard, began proceedings by giving Miss Radford a shot of morphia. Forty minutes later her broken ankle was set, and she was peacefully asleep with Maggie watching at her side. Knapp, grateful to find a Lucullan feast awaiting him in the upstairs sitting room, sat down at the bridge table with the Hunters and Clara.

"You folks are mighty kind and pleasant about this," he said, "and as far as Alvira Radford's concerned there isn't a thing to worry about. She's had a shock, but she's a strong, tough woman. I hate to send you in for that codeine and luminal, Hunter, but if she comes out of the morphia—I don't think she will—she'll need it before morning. Trouble is, somebody ought to sit up with her."

"We ought to be able to manage that among the four of us," said Hunter.

"Mighty nice of you. I could get Mrs. Simms up, perhaps."

"Let Mrs. Simms have her sleep; she probably needs it a good deal more than we do."

Clara said: "She mustn't be left alone a minute—not a minute. I dragged her in here; she didn't want to come."

Knapp paused with his coffee cup halfway to his mouth. Then he said: "She won't know anything about it till morning."

"Oughtn't we to move her into the other downstairs bedroom, Dr. Knapp? That one's so near the kitchen and bathroom; she may hear noises."

"She won't hear a thing, and she can't be moved tonight." Knapp again looked at her. Then he said: "I'll have to get hold of that Sam of hers. He'll have to tie up those dogs, if the stretcher's to get into the house tomorrow, and I'm not so anxious to be chewed up myself. I'll have to get hold of somebody to look after her; she'd rather be at home, and the hospital's choke-full anyway. Old fellows like me are getting run off our legs. How did the accident happen, Mrs. Gamadge? Did she try to turn short? There's no cut-under to those old buggies."

"The horse was frightened at something, and tipped her over." Clara went on, rather quickly: "I was thinking— oughtn't we to notify the Grobys?"

"Oh dear," said Fanny. "Won't tomorrow do?"

"Not much love lost there," said Knapp, "but it might be just as well to give them a ring. I wouldn't want Walt Groby to think he had anything on *me*."

"Perhaps they'll insist on moving her," said Clara.

This time Knapp allowed her to hold his gaze. He said at last: "She lived on in this cottage a month after her sister died, Mrs. Gamadge; don't you worry about Alvira, she's just like all the rest of the country folks—hates to be sick out of her own home."

Fanny said, rather uncomfortably, "I think Clara thinks the cottage might have unpleasant associations for Miss Radford."

"Now, my dear," expostulated Hunter; and Knapp, somewhat crossly, remarked: "Stuff. She lived here a month afterwards. Well, I'd better be moving."

"I'll go along on foot," said Hunter. "Tow the old horse down, and help you rout out the hired man. Then I'll come back and get the car and drive in for the medicine."

Knapp drove slowly down the dark road, Hunter leading old Bill ten paces to the rear. Clara and Fanny washed dishes, while Maggie kept her watch at the bedside. It had already been settled that she, at least, should get to bed promptly at ten o'clock. She had her work to do in the morning.

After a time Hunter was heard starting his car, and Clara told Fanny Hunter that she felt like crying. "You're just angels, Fanny, that's all."

"Darling, we love helping you. It was an awful upset."

"I'll get the Herons' room ready for you and Mr. Hunter."

"If you go on calling him that he says he'll feel too old to sit up and take care of Miss Radford."

"I do think she hates being here, Fanny."

"And Dr. Knapp knows it! But what can we do? As he says, she probably won't even be conscious before morning."

Hunter returned, and delivered his package to Clara. "There you are," he said. "One of each if she wakes up. Come on out on the porch." Under stress, Clara was amused to note, his little affectations of speech and manner departed; he was efficient, cool and practical.

When they were all sitting on the bench and smoking, he outlined his plan for the night:

"Now I know you two well enough to know that you won't let me do what I want—put a comfortable chair outside Alvira's door, have a good lamp, and spend the next eight hours contentedly reading, perhaps working. It's nothing to me; I like the small hours."

"Sit up from ten o'clock to six in the morning? I never heard anything so frightful," exclaimed Clara. "It's my cottage, and Miss Radford's my landlady. I won't have it."

"What is your suggestion?"

Clara had been thinking. "We might all play cards very quietly until twelve, and then you could sit up till dawn, and I'd take over after that."

"Certainly not. I demand the graveyard stretch, and I don't in the least recommend sitting up and playing cards until twelve. We must all get some sleep. Fanny can sit up till twelve—with the lamp and the chair and the book, you know; you can sit up till two, and I will be responsible for the rest of the night. I'll call Maggie in the morning."

Fanny said: "I don't care how long I sit up, but you must sleep in the other little downstairs room."

"I had no intention of sleeping anywhere else."

Clara again felt like crying—this time from relief. She said: "I should have died without you and Fanny; just died!"

"After all," continued Fanny plaintively, "it isn't as if Miss Radford were an ordinary patient; I mean some people think she's a murderer!"

"Put that stuff out of your mind, put it right out!" Hunter addressed his wife sternly. "It's nonsense, it always was nonsense." He consulted his watch. "Five of ten; Clara, you and I must soon bid Fanny good night."

"Oh, Heavens, I forgot the Grobys!" Clara went into the living room, and found the Grobys' number; Mr. Groby answered in a tone of boredom—he evidently did not recognize Clara's voice, and was bored by his wife's friends. He went away and got Mrs. Groby, who sounded impatient.

"Yes? What is it? What is it?"

Clara explained that Miss Radford had had an accident.

"An accident!" screamed Mrs. Groby.

"Yes, her ankle is broken, but she's going to be all right. We have her here in the cottage, and Dr. Knapp's seen her, and he'll have her moved to the farm in the morning."

"My goodness, Mrs. Gamadge, Walter and I had better come out."

"You really needn't, Mrs. Groby; the Hunters are here with me, and we're taking good care of her."

"What on earth happened to her?"

"The buggy tipped over."

"Well, I think you're being fine about it, and we have this party here—supper and bridge; but Aunt Alvira won't like it if we—"

"She's sound asleep under morphia. She probably won't wake up till morning."

Clara thought there was a slight scuffle at the other end of the wire; but Mrs. Groby kept hold of the telephone. She said: "I'd insist on coming, if we didn't have these friends."

At this point Mr. Groby evidently succeeded in shoving his wife aside. He spoke with polite deference: "Good evening, Mrs. Gamadge. This is a kind of a mix-up for you, from what I can hear."

"Not at all. There are four of us—"

"Mighty kind of the Hunters; mighty kind. Tell him we appreciate it. We sort of feel that my wife's place is at her aunt's bedside; are you sure there are no complications?"

"Dr. Knapp says not, but of course she'll have a thorough examination tomorrow."

"I'd drive Hattie out, party or no party, but they're business friends; it's business for me. Would it be too much to ask you not to tell Alvira that you called us?"

Clara was somewhat taken aback. "Not tell her?"

"In the morning. She's a little sensitive—touchy."

"Oh, I see. I won't mention it unless she asks."

"Well, thanks for everything; see you in the morning."

Clara, rather annoyed, went into the dining room to find Hunter placing a lamp on the end of the table, not six feet from the bedroom door. She said: "They want me to take the blame for their not coming out tonight."

"Of course they do," said Hunter cheerfully. He brought an easy chair from the living room, and placed it parallel to the sick-room door. "There we are. Light placed so that it doesn't shine in on her, chair placed so that we can see her by turning our heads. Snug as you please; we can write letters, do a jigsaw puzzle, compose poetry."

Mrs. Hunter came down the dining-room stairway, in one of Clara's dressing gowns. She said: "I'm all ready."

"You won't be lonely," asked Clara, "sleeping upstairs? One of us will be right down here, and you know Maggie's right at the top of the stairway outside your bedroom."

"Of course I shan't be lonely, and while we're here Phin will be just around the corner."

Maggie was sent to bed. Clara tilted the shade of the little lamp beside Miss Radford's bed so that her face was in shadow, placed the two boxes of capsules ready, and got fresh drinking water. She settled Fanny to her book, left a sweater for her shoulders in case it should turn cool later, and a sweater for her feet, and joined Hunter in the living room.

"I've made the rounds again upstairs," he told her, "and locked all the doors. The window screens are pretty tight; we'll all hear it if anybody tampers with *them*."

"Oh, thank you, Phin. I don't know *how* to thank you."

"I have an idea that that woman in the sunbonnet is badly on your nerves."

"She isn't now."

"Look here; would you like a shakedown on this decent-looking sofa? Instead of going up to your own room for this two-hour nap you're going to have?"

"I meant to sneak down after you were safely shut up in your room. I was ashamed to tell you and Fanny."

"Sh. Fanny needn't know." His dark, humorous face smiled down at her. "Get your things. I won't be more than a few steps away; you can doze in peace."

She rushed upstairs, dragged bedding off the bed, got into a bathrobe, and was back again. Hunter helped her to make up the sofa, and then, with a parting wave of encouragement, went into the blue room and shut the door.

This was better than she had hoped. She peeped around the edge of the door at Fanny, who was apparently quite comfortable, absorbed in her book; then she lay down on the sofa, her watch under the pillow. It seemed only a minute or two before she was waked by the sound of Fanny getting out of her chair.

She went into the dining room. Fanny, looking sleepy, was surprised to see her.

"Why, Clara, can you wake yourself? I was just going to call you."

"I didn't want you to sit up beyond your time."

"No danger of that!" Fanny laughed softly. "I should have been asleep in a minute. I went in twice to look at her; she's all right."

"Well, here's your candle now." Clara lighted one. "You've done your share—ever so much more than your share. I'd go up with you, but I hate to leave her, even for a minute."

"There's one thing—if you get frightened, you won't have to call very loud to wake Phin, or any of us!"

"No."

Fanny climbed the stairs to her landing. Clara went into the little green bedroom; she had no intention, had never had any intention of keeping her watch outside its door; she meant to keep it in the wicker chair beside the night table. If Miss Radford should open her eyes, she would know in one moment that Clara was there.

The bed was placed along the east wall, under the screened window, and facing the door that went nowhere. This presented a front as blank and solid as the wall, and no less reassuring. Miss Radford was sleeping calmly, her face turned away from the light; Clara tilted the shade a little more, to cast her deeper in shadow and give herself plenty of light for her crossword puzzle. She sat down and opened the book.

But she could not concentrate on her puzzle; she could not look away from the bony profile on the pillow, yellow against white; from the little gauze and plaster patch on the scratched and wrinkled cheek, the thin ridge of nose, the deep eye socket. She could not help listening to Miss Radford's deep breaths. She could not help wondering what Miss Radford's dreams were, if murder had really been committed in this room twelve months before.

I have a neurosis, she thought. If Henry were here he would laugh at me; there are no ghosts. That woman in the sunbonnet probably lives in the Simms attic, and gets out now and then; you hear of such things—feeble-minded relatives the family keeps locked up and won't tell about. There's more than one purple dress and sunbonnet in the world, and Maggie tinkers with the attic door and then forgets she left it open.

Well, one thing was certain; Clara wasn't going to give in and talk about ghosts to Phineas Hunter; that was something you never lived down. How mortifying for Gamadge, to have people saying that his wife was weak in the head.

She applied herself seriously to her puzzle, and worked at it for what seemed to her a long time. Her watch said twenty minutes past twelve, then half past twelve, then twenty minutes to one. She felt thirsty, thought of going to the kitchen for ice water, and suddenly realized that she was afraid to get up and walk out into the lighted dining room. She was afraid to move from her chair.

I've read about this, she thought. This is what happens to people who sit up all night in a haunted house; it gets them. Anything can happen. People don't wake when you call, or they're all dead.

She was still gazing at her watch, which seemed to have stopped; or had all these thoughts rushed through her mind in a few seconds, and was it still twenty minutes to one? There was a small sound like something dropping to the floor, and she raised her eyes in time to see the sealed door swing open, pushed by a brownish hand at the end of an arm clad in faded purple. It was there, against a screen of darkness; shapeless and faceless in its black-sprigged garment and its collapsed sunbonnet, it seemed to dominate the room.

If it comes in I shall go out of my mind, thought Clara. I shall go out of my mind if I see its face. But it did not come in, it was there only a moment; it faded or moved aside, it was no longer in the doorway; it had retreated as if before Clara's presence, as if unable to enter the room while she sat staring at it.

For a few seconds Clara's head went forward almost to her knees; then the dizziness left her, and with her eyes again on the black oblong of the doorway she struggled to her feet. Still watching the empty place where the figure had stood, she walked stiffly to the door that led into the dining room; there, clinging to the frame, she tried to scream for Hunter. His door was shut, but somebody must hear her. She screamed wildly.

She thought she would never hear sounds in the house, but at last Hunter came at a run through the living room. In his shirt sleeves and his black dress-trousers, what did he look like? A duelist? He was across the dining room in two seconds, and had her by the elbows; she clutched him, her eyes still on the blackness beyond the open door.

"Clara—what is it?" He was staring over her shoulder at that incredible gateway to mystery and night.

"She came, she came! The woman in the sunbonnet!"

"Who opened that door?"

"She did."

He frowned, and turned his head to the left.

"She's all right," gasped Clara. "The woman didn't come in. Miss Radford's all right."

But Hunter, still looking at the bed, was frowning even more heavily. He asked: "Will you be all right for a moment? You won't fall?"

"No."

He left her leaning against the doorframe, and went past her and up to the bedside. Clara, watching him, saw him stand there, looking down; saw him bend slightly, saw his face change. Then he just put out a hand and touched

Miss Radford's, which lay along the counterpane. He turned and came back to Clara.

"Come out of here, my poor child."

"We can't leave her! We must fasten that door shut!"

"Nothing can hurt her now."

"Phineas—you don't mean... She was all right!"

"She's dead. She's been killed."

"That thing never came into the room. I never took my eyes off it or off the doorway except for a few seconds when I got dizzy, nothing could have happened in just those seconds, I should have known." Her words were running together. Hunter got her into the dining room, into the easy chair. Fanny came running down, Maggie lumbered in her wake.

"Get her some whiskey, you two," Clara heard him say. "Get her to bed. Wait a minute, give her some of the luminal with the whiskey. I'll get it."

"I'll get it," said Maggie's voice.

"No, don't go in there. Nobody must—I must telephone."

He dashed into the bedroom and out again, the little box of tablets in his hand. Then Clara found herself being helped up the stairs, heard Hunter telephoning, heard herself ask the time over and over again—she didn't know why. Somebody told her that it was thirteen minutes to one.

Things became confused for Clara. She was put to bed in her own room, she had whiskey and luminal, somebody sat beside her, holding her hand, until she fell asleep.

6

Gamadge Does Not Laugh

Gamadge's plane arrived in Canada on Monday, July the sixth. He reached Washington late that night, reported at headquarters, and then tried to get Clara by telephone. He was told that the number did not answer, growled invective against rural telephone services, and sent a telegram giving the address of his hotel. He said that he would be with her on Wednesday.

Three letters were waiting for him in the office; he waved off a dozen people while he read them, frowning a little at the last one; it was dated Wednesday the first, and told him that Clara was alone with Maggie in the cottage. Well, he was more than ever glad that he had been able to get home ahead of schedule.

He at last got to the hotel, and by one A.M. began to wonder whether the Connecticut telegraph system had broken down also. But it was late to call Clara, or try to call her; he finally decided to wait until morning.

At seven he was awakened by the reply to his telegram, which said:

YOUR TELEGRAM DELAYED WE ARE AT HUNTERS MOUNTAIN RIDGE FARM LET US KNOW WHEN TO MEET YOU DO NOT WORRY WHEN YOU SEE PAPERS I AM SO GLAD YOU ARE HERE LOVE

CLARA

Gamadge sent down for papers—New York and Hartford papers—and began to dress. When they arrived he was swallowing coffee. He found what he was looking for on an inside page:

Avebury, Conn.—No new light has been thrown on the strange death of Miss Alvira Radford of North Avebury, who was found strangled to death on the morning of Sunday, July 5th. The inquest has been adjourned. Miss Radford owned the cottage where she met her death. She had rented it for the summer to Mr. and Mrs. Richard Heron of Longport, Long Island, and Mr. and Mrs. Henry Gamadge of New York City. She had been carried into the cottage after a buggy accident on Saturday afternoon, July 4th, by Mrs. Gamadge and her maid Miss Maggie Shearn, who were living alone there. At the time of the murder Mr. and Mrs. Phineas Hunter of Mountain Ridge Farm and New York City were also in the cottage. Mrs. Gamadge was sitting up with Miss Radford when as she alleges a strange woman entered the bedroom and strangled the victim. Mrs. Gamadge states that she did not actually see the murder committed, and that she could not identify the murderer, as her face was concealed. State's Attorney Ledwell, of Stratfield, Conn., states that Mrs. Gamadge's testimony is confused.

The killer has been seen in the neighborhood, according to Mrs. Gamadge and Miss Shearn, for several days past. No clues have been found as to her identity. Mrs. Gamadge is staying until after the inquest with Mr. and Mrs. Hunter. She is said to be still prostrated.

Gamadge, his eyes still glued to these paragraphs, reached for the telephone. He dictated a telegram:

MRS. HENRY GAMADGE, CARE HUNTER, MOUNTAIN RIDGE FARM, NORTH AVEBURY, CONN.
WILL BE WITH YOU TODAY DO NOT KNOW WHEN LOVE TO YOU AND REGARDS TO HUNTERS

HENRY

He got an answer before he had finished stuffing things into the smaller of his two bags:

SO GLAD DO NOT WORRY I AM ALL RIGHT NOW KNEW YOU WOULD COME

CLARA

Gamadge did not have time to telephone. He does not know to this day how he caught the train that got him to New York in time to catch the three o'clock for Hartford; but he managed before he left Washington to order his other bag sent after him, to see his chief, and to get a fortnight's leave. During the two-and-a-half hour's run to Hartford he reread Clara's letters and the paragraphs on Miss Radford's peculiar death, but none of them told him anything new.

At Hartford he caught a bus to Avebury—fourteen miles of delightful country which he did not appreciate. At Avebury he hired a car and a driver, and reached Mountain Ridge Farm just as Phineas Hunter, wishing for the departed Alonzo, was shaking cocktails for dinner.

Hunter put down the shaker when Maggie, wild with excitement announced the guest. He rushed into the hall and shouted for Clara, meanwhile shaking Gamadge's hand and pounding his shoulder. Clara flew down the stairs and into her husband's arms. The taximan, waiting in the front doorway with Gamadge's bag, got a good look at Mrs. Gamadge; he wondered what was behind the Radford killing, and whether he was really gazing at a society strangler.

Gamadge somehow paid him. Fanny Hunter arrived, pushed the Gamadges towards the stairs, and told them that dinner would be kept back; they had three-quarters of an hour.

Gamadge had to use some of this precious time to wash and shave; but Clara, who looked less battle-worn than he did, stood beside him and handed him things. It would take a good deal, he thought, to make a wreck of Clara. But that she had had an ordeal was plain enough, and as he looked at her he thought it had been a worse one than she as yet wanted him to guess. She said: "Henry..."

"Yes, my angel?"

"Henry, could we just not talk about it tonight? About Miss Radford, or anything?"

"I don't want to talk about Miss Radford—if you don't."

"It's so wonderful, having you back. I can't bear to spoil it."

"You couldn't spoil it."

"Yes, I could." She stood beside him in her white dress, a towel over her arm, his comb and brush in her hands. "You'll be—it's all so dreadful. Much worse than people know."

"Do just as you like about telling me. Tell me now, if you'd rather."

"You aren't like anybody else; you haven't even asked me a question."

"No, but I'm dying to; I want to know whether you choked this Miss Radford to death in a moment of antipathy."

Clara laughed wildly. "You always know just what to say!"

"Glad you think so."

"I knew I shouldn't have to explain to *you* that I may be arrested."

"I'm only too thankful you're not in jail."

"The Hunters are too important; they just did everything for me. And then of course I had no motive."

"Unless you had run up a terrific bill for eggs and chickens, and couldn't pay." He added, putting his razor down, "I know what you must have been through, my darling. I think your idea was a very sound one—about postponing the whole thing until tomorrow. This is a reunion."

"It isn't what it would have been if we were in the cottage. It's all ruined for you."

"Ruined? I have no time to tell you now whether it's ruined or not. I must get dressed for dinner."

At dinner the Gamadges were allowed to sit side by side, with the Hunters opposite across a small gate table. This was placed in the great bay of the dining room, which rode like a ship above the valley. There seemed to be quite enough to talk about without any references, on the part of anyone, to the tragedy and all that it had brought in its wake; and by the time Clara had had a glass of dry champagne, the cure begun by Gamadge's first telegram was completed; her natural color came back, and the look that Gamadge had been dismayed to see in her eyes left them, not to return.

After dinner, while they were having coffee and brandy in the yellow room, Gilbert Craye was announced. Hunter was for having him sent home, but Gamadge said he should like to see him. He came in, was immensely surprised to find Gamadge there, shook hands violently all around, and—catching the spirit of the occasion—uttered no word of the tragedy. Perhaps he had come to condole with Clara, but he remained to sing. Fanny played, and he sang classic airs; then, at her request, he sat down and accompanied himself to airs that were not classic. When he left, Clara was in a pleasant half-dream.

"I do think," said Fanny, when they were all saying good night, "that it was horrid of you, Phin; to make up that thing about Gil Craye flitting like a fly, you know."

"Because of his pleasing tenor?" Hunter smiled down at her. "Because the small gnats mourn?"

"What's all this?" asked Gamadge.

Hunter repeated his couplet, and Gamadge was highly entertained by it.

"I was tempted beyond my strength," said Hunter. "Shocking thing. Bad enough to have composed it, worse to repeat it; *you* mustn't."

Gamadge said: "Clara and I are putting off the affair Radford until tomorrow; and until tomorrow I shall put off trying to thank you and Fanny for all you've done for her; I imagine that I don't know half of it."

Fanny protested: "We didn't do half enough! We should all have sat up. She shouldn't have been left alone."

"You were alone, Fanny." Clara spoke in a low voice.

"Yes, but I didn't sit right there in that awful room!"

"Tomorrow, tomorrow," Gamadge urged his wife up the stairs.

"Tomorrow," said Hunter, "you'll find out that your wife's a thoroughbred."

"Shall I?" Gamadge looked at Clara and smiled.

Next morning, down on the flat rock beside the Ladder trail, where she had taken him to hear the story, he listened in silence; asked her to repeat it, from her first view of the woman in the sunbonnet to her last conscious thought on Sunday morning after the tragedy; questioned her minutely on each smallest detail, and then repeated Hunter's words: "You're a thoroughbred."

"I was afraid you'd laugh at me for being so—for thinking it was a ghost."

"Laugh? The chain of evidence was reinforced progressively by every link. It's an appalling story, and as queer a one as I ever heard in my life. Now let's tackle it from the other point of view—the rationalist's point of view. You can do that now, since you're no longer on the spot."

"That's what I want to do."

"We'll make notes. I borrowed a pad from Fanny." Gamadge produced the pad and a pencil. "What a raving beauty she is, by the way. Craye's in love with her."

"Is he?" Clara was startled.

"But perhaps he flits from lady to lady, and it means nothing serious. I had a talk with Hunter this morning; he says they got a sworn statement from you on Sunday for the inquest, now adjourned."

"Yes; I was in bed. Phineas was wonderful, but of course I had to see everybody on Monday. I felt all right, and I got up. The sheriff of Avebury came—a very nice man. He says it must have been an escaped lunatic, and that's what he put in the papers; but he doesn't know what to think, any more than I do."

"How much did you tell him?"

"Only what actually happened. I didn't mention the things in the attic, or the attic door. Should I have?"

Gamadge put his hand on hers. "My poor child, what an infernal time you've had; some women would have lost their wits."

"I nearly did that night, when I looked up and saw the door opening."

"After you heard something drop."

"Like a piece of wood, a small piece."

"Did you mention that to the sheriff?"

"Yes."

"But you managed to conceal the entire ghost angle?"

"I was afraid he'd think *I* was the lunatic."

Gamadge, his eyes on her profile, set his teeth. After a moment he spoke lightly: "Just as well not to give them the impression that you're fanciful. You'll have to testify at this confounded inquest, and you want them to feel that you have your wits about you."

"Yes, but how can they think I have my wits about me? Because how could that woman have killed Miss Radford when she never even came into the room?"

"I know."

"They all want me to say I fainted when I saw her, but I didn't faint. I saw her at twenty minutes to one, and when they took me upstairs it was thirteen minutes to; only seven minutes! I didn't have time to faint."

"Perhaps they think you made a mistake when you looked at your watch."

"I didn't. It was twenty minutes to one, and I wondered how I could stand another hour and twenty minutes of it. I thought I'd have to call Phineas Hunter, and say I was frightened, and tell him everything."

"Well, let's leave the problem and tackle something else. About the dress and the sunbonnet; could you swear that they were the ones you saw in the attic?"

"Yes, I could. I was sure of the color even before I saw her close up, and on Saturday afternoon, and later, in the bedroom doorway, I saw the black sprigs."

"You described the material to the sheriff?"

"Yes, and to the state's attorney from Stratfield and the captain of the state police. Mr. Ledwell—the state's attorney—was very polite; he's quite a young man, and I could see that he was dying to go on asking me questions until he made sense of the case. But Phineas wouldn't let him stay more than an hour. He was terribly puzzled, and quite irritated; I don't blame him. He made me say again and again that I never heard of Miss Radford till I got here, and didn't know at first that she owned the cottage, and thought she was only the egg-woman. And I told him how Dick Heron had made the arrangements with an agent in Hartford. He kept doing what he called checking up; he checked up with Phineas Hunter, and he called up the agent, and he called Dick. He seemed quite pleased— told me I was fully corroborated," said Clara, with a dim smile.

"Just his precious routine."

"Phineas Hunter was wonderful; so polite to them, but right in the offing. I could see that they didn't like to offend him, but what can they do? They have to try and find out what happened."

"Tell you what; if we don't dig something up for them, we'll have Bob Macloud here for the inquest. We'll give him a watching brief," said Gamadge, in a jocular tone. "Nobody can overstep legal propriety with Bob in a courtroom."

"I don't think they want to overstep it. Oh—I forgot; they had their own doctor—the medical examiner—to look me over."

Gamadge slowly pushed the end of his walking stick into the hard turf between his feet. After a pause he asked: "What for?"

"Well, to find out about whether I often faint, and whether I have lapses of memory, or lapses of consciousness, or anything. He took notes about my putting my head down because I felt dizzy. I told him every illness I ever had, and every illness I ever heard of in the family."

Gamadge waited still longer before he put his next question: "How long was your head down?"

"I ought to know by this time, I've thought of it so much! It may have been thirty seconds; ten to get it down, and ten to keep it down, and ten to get it up again."

"Not long enough."

"I know it; but they say that I must have rushed to the door and stood there calling Phineas Hunter without looking behind me at what was going on in the room. I didn't. I never looked away from that open doorway once. She never came back."

"Hunter says you were looking at it when he came, and that it was the first thing he saw, of course."

"And then he looked at Miss Radford, and knew that something had happened to her. The state police-captain was so puzzled about it all that he was quite cross at first. I don't think he likes summer people much; I suppose they give him a lot of trouble with their cars and accidents. He wanted to know what we had to drink during the evening."

"Poor fellow, his life is one long pursuit of the fumes of alcohol, I suppose."

"Phineas mixed cocktails for us at supper. Dr. Knapp did enjoy his so. The state police-captain thought I might have been asleep all evening, and dreamed the woman. But then, who could have murdered Miss Radford?"

"I gather that he wasn't cerebrating actively, or hadn't heard the rest of the story; they know there was a woman, Maggie saw her."

"I think they think perhaps I made her up later—thought I saw her, I mean, but didn't. They don't know what to think, Henry."

"They know perfectly well that you're telling the truth as you know it."

"Yes, but—they make me feel so crazy. The state police-captain was rather impatient with me, but Fanny came in with iced coffee and chocolate cakes, and he had some. That's a good sign, isn't it?"

Gamadge said: "What I mean is, the idiots must see that if you wanted to make up a story you could, and that it would satisfy them all. You could simply say that you did faint."

"Yes, and because I don't say so they think I'm crazy."

Gamadge opened Fanny's pad and placed it on his knee. "Let's tackle the thing in our own way. We'll put it in the form of a story, you know, and the story will have a beginning, a middle and an end. It begins on July the sixth, 1941."

"But that's when I began it! That's when the ghost story begins!"

"My story begins there too."

7

Another Point of View

"Until Sunday afternoon, July sixth, 1941," began Gamadge, "Alvira Radford and her sister Eva Hickson occupied what had once been their farm cottage. The farm itself was down the road, on the other side of the highway; it had been rented, it had been mortgaged, and it now stood empty. Alvira Radford, a woman of small means, had lived in the cottage for economy's sake since—Hunter thinks—1932; Mrs. Hickson joined her some years later, after Hickson died. Alvira does not seem to have known much about Hickson, or Mrs. Hickson's married life; since, if gossip is to be believed, she did not know until Mrs. Hickson's death that that lady had possessed what to Alvira must have seemed a great fortune—one hundred and six thousand dollars.

"Mrs. Hickson, a victim of arthritis, had for some time occupied a downstairs bedroom. This bedroom may at one time have been an entry; it had an outer door, now closed up against drafts. After her death Miss Radford did not have this door opened, and refused her summer tenant's suggestion that it should be opened; her objection being that the process might mar the new paint.

"Late in the afternoon of July sixth, Mrs. Hickson died. She had been ailing for a couple of weeks with what has been vaguely described by a neighbor as gastric stomach, and we do not know whether her doctor expected her to die or not; but although he was not at the cottage when death took place, he gave a certificate. Mrs. Hickson was buried handsomely in Avebury old cemetery, where I suppose her forebears lie.

"Miss Radford stayed on at the cottage for a month after the death; but (having learned that she was sole heir to her sister's money) she immediately ordered repairs and improvements at the farm. These alterations, or what can be seen of them, are in the worst taste; but after moving back to the farm she ordered improvements made at the cottage which are all in very good taste indeed. The local builder was not given a free hand here; somebody was engaged who knew the kind of thing that summer tenants would like. Valuable old furniture was left behind, and a new kitchen wing put on; but the original charm was preserved, and the little place unspoiled.

"Part of its charm consisted in the oddity of its still being—outdoors as well as in—a double cottage. Although its only ground-floor back door had been condemned, it had a back door on the hillside, and no less than three front ones. It had two enclosed stairways, one from the living room and one from the dining room, and two attics. One of these had been fitted up as a bedroom, and ceiled.

"In the other one, the one above the north bedroom, Miss Radford left her sister's possessions—all of them, we guess; the things she had worn, the things she had treasured, the furniture she had brought back from her married home. We shall not be straining conjecture if we conclude that when Alvira Radford left the cottage she meant to leave behind her every possible memory of the sister, all her effects, even the family furniture which they had used in common. The only thing she retained of Mrs. Hickson's was Mrs. Hickson's money.

"After setting up at the farm she became a recluse to the extent of putting up a wire fence, purchasing two large and fierce watchdogs, and never going to church. We do not know whether these innovations followed, or are partly responsible for, the rumor which soon spread locally—that Mrs. Hickson had not died of gastric trouble, but of arsenic. I say arsenic, of course, since arsenic is a poison familiar in country usage, procurable for country uses, and well known to produce symptoms resembling gastric disease. If the rumor spread immediately after Mrs. Hickson's death, I can very well understand that Miss Alvira Radford would not go to church to be stared at; for I think it very doubtful that she should not have heard what her kind neighbors were saying.

"But was there any rumor of a haunting? Was Mrs. Hickson's ghost known to walk?"

"No, I'm sure Web Hawley or Mrs. Simms would have let it out if there had been."

"So far as you know, you and Maggie—and Miss Radford herself, on the day of the accident—are the only persons who ever saw the woman in the sunbonnet. Quite naturally, since you and Maggie are the first persons to have lived there since Alvira Radford vacated it; vacated it, you have been tempted to fear, because she had seen the woman in the sunbonnet, only too often.

"At any rate, you yourself are sure that Alvira disliked the place, wouldn't set foot in it, and rather preferred you to think that she wasn't the owner.

"Meanwhile you were disturbed by the appearance, every three days and at sunset, of a woman in a sunbonnet;

and by the fact that shortly after each appearance the door to the north attic was found open. You investigated the attic, and there discovered evidence that connected Miss Radford, through her sister, with the manifestations. Later, when on two occasions you saw the woman at close quarters, you were completely convinced that the garments worn by her, and the garments you had found in the attic, were the same. You were convinced that all these happenings were related—parts of a ghastly whole. You were right."

Clara, her eyes fixed anxiously on his face, said nothing.

"But let us try," continued Gamadge, "to bring the matter out of the realms of the supernatural and down to earth. We can hope to do so only by inquiring into Miss Radford's character and into her past. We must ignore the whole fabric of evidence as it was presented to you, and account in some other way for what you were meant to look upon as unaccountable.

"In the first place: there are more reasons than one for shaking the dust of a place off one's feet; and fear of the place is not the commonest reason. Let's assume that Miss Radford and her rich (and miserly) sister didn't get on.

"In the second place: though human instinct leads people unreasonably enough to put up material bars against malignant spirits, there are better reasons for fences and watchdogs. Perhaps Miss Radford also had the miser instinct; perhaps she liked to keep some of her wealth in the house with her, where she could look at it.

"She struggled against being carried into the house on Saturday, after her accident; no wonder! She had just seen what she could only suppose to be the ghost of her dead sister, and she had fainted at the sight; from what you tell me, I think she must have fainted before the buggy went over."

"Yes, the reins were tangled up anyhow—she had dropped them."

"Of course she fainted; and when she came to, dazed from shock, she remembered what she had seen, protested against being kept in precincts that she could only think haunted, and fainted again. I don't blame her. But you say she quieted down afterwards?"

"Yes."

"If she had poisoned Mrs. Hickson, and just seen her

avenging ghost, she would have raised the roof; made such a row that Knapp would have had to get her out of there on a stretcher. At any rate, she wouldn't have quieted down and taken a shot of morphia like a lamb, with the powers of darkness, for all she knew, closing in on her. She had seen a ghost, but not an avenging ghost."

"I'm sure Dr. Knapp had heard the rumor about the poisoning."

"And Eli has heard it."

"Has he? He told me there was nothing to be afraid of here but copperheads!"

Gamadge said: "I'd rather you'd met a copperhead."

"Than—than the woman in the sunbonnet?"

"You ran up against something that didn't wait to be hurt or interfered with before it attacked you viciously. If the attic door was open every time you saw the woman, it was the woman who opened it; it could have been closed, it was left open to frighten you. Anybody could have come and gone by those doors and stairways without being seen by you or Maggie, couldn't they?"

"I suppose so."

"Think it over, and you'll know so; for it must have happened. Out of doors there must be plenty of cover; we'll go down and look.

"Now for the inquiry into Miss Radford's own life. She profited by her sister's death; who profits by hers?"

"Why, if she didn't will the money away from them, Mrs. Groby. The Grobys are rich!"

"Mrs. Groby, from your account of her, seems to possess a frivolous disposition, and a husband who is short on principle. Miss Radford is said not to have cared much for the Grobys, and when they heard of her accident they did not behave as though they cared much for her. The Grobys had better have effective alibis for Saturday afternoon and the early hours of Sunday morning."

"They were having a party."

"But when did it begin and end? We may be sure that the sheriff, the captain of state police, and the state's attorney of Stratfield are looking into the matter.

"We have one other faint suggestion as to the character of Alvira Radford, and it helps to keep us out of the realm of the supernatural, and on solid earth. When Gilbert Craye brought you the stuff on Friday afternoon he made a mistake about Miss Radford which interests me very much. At least, you say that he had a talk with you in the course of which you found yourselves at cross-purposes. You thought he was referring to the rumor that Miss Radford had poisoned her sister; but you found that he had never heard the rumor, and was thinking of something else— something which seemed to have set him against her. When you asked him what it was, he turned the conversation."

"I thought he meant that she and those friends of hers in Stratfield had been gossiping about him."

"And from whom would you have heard this, if not from Miss Radford herself? You had only two other sources of information—the Simms outfit, and the Hunters. I should not suppose that Mrs. Simms and her hired man know anything whatever about Gilbert Craye, who lives ten miles off in Stratfield; and the Hunters, presumably, should not repeat gossip about him."

"They never repeated any, and neither did Mrs. Simms or Web Hawley."

"But Miss Radford has friends in Stratfield. However, it's all very vague at present, and I only mention it as an indication that Alvira Radford had enemies on the earthly plane."

"Gilbert Craye!"

"We mustn't neglect what we have. Clara—" he turned, and put an arm around her shoulders, "have I managed to explode the ghost theory for you?"

"You've convinced me that there was no ghost. I knew you would!"

"If I've done that, I've done something of vast importance to this investigation."

"Of course the woman could have gone and got those clothes—and put them back in the attic. It's pretty awful to think that she was wandering around and hiding in the house."

"She won't come back, you know."

"But you haven't told me how she could have killed Miss Radford, when I was right there and awake!"

"Never mind how she killed Miss Radford. What I want is to get you to do me a colossal favor."

"You know I'll do anything."

"I want you to come back with me and live at the cottage."

Clara's gray eyes met his green ones in a long look. She said at last: "Maggie will never go there again."

"You're wrong. She said this morning that she would if you would. She figures that the cottage isn't haunted any more—Mrs. Hickson has had her revenge, you know, and can rest in peace."

"I can't believe that Maggie will go back!"

"She's promised to, if we want her. I told her that she should sleep in the Herons' bedroom, with all doors open; and I only hope she doesn't snore."

"Of course I'll go anywhere you want me to. It will be all right if you're there."

"That's talking." He pressed her hard against his side. "I knew you would. Now I'll explain why I'm so keen on going. In the first place, I quite agree with Maggie that the hauntings are over; their object has certainly been accomplished. They certainly weren't engineered just to frighten you away. There are no counterfeiters' dens or smugglers' caves on the place, I suppose?"

Clara said there were none, so far as she knew.

"Then the attic door will stay shut from now on—unless we want it open. We'll leave the other mysterious door—the condemned one—wide open, by the way; we'll put a handle on it and give it a step. We'll take the furniture out of that bedroom, and use it as a back entry; a thing which the cottage seems to need."

"Henry, that will make all the difference!"

"The Herons' maid will have to have the other little bedroom, and we won't invite any weekend guests; or if we do, they can sleep in the upstairs sitting room."

"There's a nice sofa there."

"And now I'll give you my reasons for wanting to go back. First, of course, to relieve the hospitable Hunters of our presence. They'll object; but after all, they may have plans for other guests."

"I've worried awfully about settling down on them."

"Naturally you have. But if we moved, where should we go if not to the cottage? I doubt if there's anything we could stand in Avebury, and even that's too far for me. That brings me to the next, and a much more important reason for a return; I want to be on the spot. In the next few days I shall have to see a lot of people and come and go at my own hours. At the cottage I shall not only be free, but halfway between Avebury and Stratfield; or at least at a strategic point between them."

"Stratfield? I simply can't believe," said Clara, distressed, "that Gilbert Craye knows anything about it!"

"He knows something about Miss Radford that he doesn't want other people to know. What was that you said he asked you, by the way, about Schenck being in the F.B.I.?"

"He just asked. I said you and Mr. Schenck didn't talk about your war work."

"I didn't know that he had ever met Schenck, or heard of him. Well, then; we come to the last reason that I can think of for settling down in the cottage, in spite of all you've been through in it; and I won't try to tell you what a sport I think you are; you know."

"It will be all right there with you."

"I've telegraphed to Dick Heron that I'm on the job, and I shall now write him a letter. I shall tell him that if he and Sally want to call the summer off, we're agreeable and shan't blame them; but that I'm going to try to clear things up, and that I hope we'll get our money's worth after all. I don't know whether I could get out of the lease, but from what you tell me of the Grobys I think I probably couldn't without a lawsuit."

"I wondered whether Dick and Sally would want to come now."

"Well, they weren't here when the thing happened; I bet if we stick it out they will. Are you sure, Clara, that you're willing to do this for me?" Again he looked at her closely; again she returned the look without wavering.

"It'll be all right with you."

"Think what a strong-minded female the sheriff, and the state's attorney, and the state police will make you out to be!" He gave her an odd smile.

"They'll all be very much surprised. I don't believe any of them would much like to live there themselves, now."

"We'll show them what we're made of. And now," he said, getting up and lifting her to her feet, "let's go down and look at the place."

They went down the Ladder; Gamadge admired every yard of the trail, and said that this kind of thing was what he had been looking forward to. Clara, watching his face, could only hope that he would succeed in enjoying himself.

8

Nobody Can Believe It

At his first view of the little yellow house half hidden by its trees, Gadmage stopped with a hand on Clara's arm. He stood absorbing the scene and tapping his stick gently against his leg; the monotone of the waterfall was in his ears, a chirping of birds, a faint rustle of leaves. Wood-smells and field-smells came to him on a cool breeze. The bend in the road cut off all sight of other human habitations.

"Do you like it?" asked Clara.

"Who wouldn't like it?"

They went on down to the beginning of the path. A state trooper got up from the porch settee and advanced upon them.

"Premises closed," he said. "Public not allowed."

"We're not public," said Gamadge. "We live here."

The trooper looked at him.

"And we have property here," continued Gamadge. "No doubt it's been protected, although I see that the yard hasn't been protected from what must have been a convention of gum chewers. We want to check up on our stuff."

The trooper asked: "You Mr. and Mrs. Gamadge?"

"Yes."

"Staying up at Hunters?"

"For the moment. We hope to move back in tonight."

"Move back in!" The trooper looked amazed.

"Certainly, move back in; why not? We have a lease."

"I didn't have any orders."

"It never occurred to me that orders were required; however, I'll speak to whoever's responsible for you. I don't understand why you should be surprised at our coming back; we've paid our advance—half the summer rental; we couldn't very well get it back, could we? Or is a murder legally considered an act of God?"

"You got me. I didn't think wild horses would get you

here." He gazed at Clara. "It's all I can do to sit on the porch."

"Psychic, are you?"

"I guess your wife isn't."

"My wife is a sensible woman. This tragedy had nothing to do with us, you know; we're thinking about our summer plans. Any objection to letting us in now? I want to be able to report on the condition of our belongings when I see the sheriff this afternoon."

The trooper hesitated. At last he said: "The new owners might want to cancel the lease."

"Who are they?"

"People named Groby. Live in Avebury; but just now they're at the farm, the Radford farm; just down on the highway."

"Thanks, I'll see them."

"They might let you off the summer rent."

"I don't know that I want to be let off. It seems a nice little place, and I haven't any wish to spend what vacation I have looking around for another one. Take us in, will you, officer?"

The trooper, after another long look at him, turned and pushed open the screen door of the living room.

"Perfectly charming," said Gamadge, standing in the middle of it with his arm by Clara's. "The decorators must be first class."

"They are," said the trooper. "Yost and Company, Hartford."

Gamadge inspected the blue bedroom, the dining room, the kitchen and the bathroom. Then he walked alone into the little green bedroom where Miss Radford had died. The blind door in the south wall hung slightly ajar, and he opened it. He looked it over with interest, and then spoke over his shoulder to the trooper, who stood with Clara in the dining room, watching him.

"This door wasn't sealed; it was just locked, and the outside metal parts taken off and painted over. The key-hole was plugged."

"So I heard," said the trooper.

"My wife heard the plug fall out before the door opened— the night Miss Radford was killed."

The trooper stared; Clara stared.

"Did they find it?" asked Gamadge, in a peremptory tone.

"I don't know," said the trooper.

"The murderer must simply have loosened it first, at some earlier time, and then pushed it through and used a key. What key? I suppose plenty of old keys would fit this old lock?"

The trooper said that the front door keys fitted it.

"The latch is loose; all the murderer had to do was to unlock the door and push." Gamadge looked down at a log which at present did duty as a step, glanced up at the new broken branches of the lilac, and then allowed his gaze to wander to the gnarled old apple trees which obscured his view of the field to the south. He stepped down and walked into the orchard. When he had a clear view of the slopes behind the cottage he stopped. The short line of the ridge stood out against the sky, the hillside beneath was like watered yellow silk across which ran a flaw—the little trail. He noted its abrupt entrance into the woods to right and left, and then turned to look at the back of the cottage. He glanced up at the attic windows, one small and dim, the other neatly curtained; at Clara's back door, just visible through trees on the slope; at the two windows on the ground floor that lighted the two little bedrooms.

Clara, looking as if she had stepped through the looking glass, came around from the ambiguous door and joined him. He smiled at her. "Let's go up to your room by the back way," he said.

They climbed over slippery dead leaves and among bushes and saplings. The trooper, toiling behind, unlocked the door for them.

Gamadge looked along the vista from Clara's room to the Herons', said it was all even nicer than he had imagined it, and then, whistling gently, went into the sitting room and climbed to the attic. When he came down he was still whistling. He stopped, to say: "All cleared out."

"I understand there was a lot of Radford stuff up there," said the trooper. "The sheriff had it carted away."

"And he carted away the plug from that keyhole. I must meet the sheriff; he seems like a very thorough man, a man I should like."

The trooper had been studying Clara unobtrusively but with concentration. Now, rather awkwardly, he said: "Mr. Gamadge, that ghost business gets in everybody's way; I mean about how the ghost could commit the murder with Mrs. Gamadge right there in the room. I got a theory that eliminates all that stuff."

"Good. Let's hear it."

"The old lady had had a shot of morphia, and I don't know if you know that it excites some people."

"I have heard that it does."

"She lays there for a while asleep; after the shock, and getting her leg set, you know; and then she wakes up. She don't know where she is, she thrashes around, gets her head up against the headboard of the bed, and breaks her neck."

Clara made a faint sound. Gamadge said hurriedly: "Go ahead."

"She's an old lady, it breaks like that." He snapped his fingers with the sound of a pistol going off. "Why, my grandmother, she broke a leg once by sitting on it; bones brittle."

"And then?" Gamadge was all attention.

"Then she slides down on the bed again of her own weight, and Mrs. Gamadge doesn't know the difference."

"Although she's on the other side of that little night table?"

"She was kind of dozing. It wouldn't take a second."

Clara said: "I wasn't dozing, and I didn't know Miss Radford's neck was broken."

"Sure, that's how she was killed." The trooper looked at her. "Didn't you know? Wouldn't take a second."

"I wasn't dozing for a second."

"You said yourself you were out for longer than that," said the trooper, almost pleadingly. "You dreamed about that woman in the sunbonnet."

"Well, officer," said Gamadge cheerfully, "we're obliged to you for the suggestion; I'm sorry my wife can't accept it. I'll drive over to Avebury this afternoon, see the sheriff, and get some of the red tape cut if I can. They'll let you know."

The trooper cleared his throat. "Will you want protection till they catch—that crazy woman?"

"No protection, thanks all the same. All I want now," said Gamadge, as they filed down the enclosed stairway, "is my car. I think it's still in the barn here."

The trooper halted. "I don't believe I can let you have that."

"Can't?" Gamadge also stopped, to look up at him in the gloom. "Why in the world not? You mean that I come up here and can't use my own car? You'd better telephone!"

The trooper telephoned. Presently he came out on the porch to say that Gamadge could have the car if Mr. Hunter would make himself responsible. "For the car," he added, "and for you and Mrs. Gamadge staying in the county."

"Call Hunter up," said Gamadge, laughing.

More telephoning resulted in a solemn assurance by Phineas Hunter that he would produce the Gamadges and their car when and if they were required. Gamadge backed his property out of the yellow barn, and he and Clara drove off in it.

Clara said: "I didn't know her neck was broken, Henry."

"Oh. Yes, it was. In the process of strangling."

"Why didn't anybody say so? Why didn't the papers say so?"

"Perhaps people thought it wasn't necessary to mention shocking details to you. As for not putting it in the papers, it will be in them after the inquest. The truth is, that poisoning story has leaked out, and the law in these parts has been in mortal horror lest the avenging ghost should leak out too."

"Why do they care?"

"Well, because they're afraid the city papers will make them out fools. Make a feature story of it, with skeleton hands clawing, you know."

"But why should Miss Radford being killed that way make the ghost leak out?"

"Well, don't you see," said Gamadge, rather reluctantly, "it was like a hanging; like an execution. That's what happens when people are hanged. Now shall we change the subject?"

They had turned up the highway, and Gamadge stopped the car at the open gate in front of the Radford farm. No dogs were anywhere in sight, and the Groby car stood just off the roadway, in the drive.

Mrs. Groby, who had probably seen the Gamadges from a window, came out of the house. She looked hot and anxious. She wore an apron over a new-looking black dress, and her hair was done up in a checked scarf. Gamadge met her halfway up the walk.

"Mrs. Groby? I'm Henry Gamadge."

"Oh, Mr. Gamadge! I didn't know you were here."

"I'm awfully sorry about your loss," he said, shaking hands.

"Thanks; but what an upset for you to run into, too! And poor Mrs. Gamadge. I hope she's feeling better?"

"She's all right again. We both hope this isn't going to make any difference in our summer plans, Mrs. Groby."

Mrs. Groby looked at him, looked past him at Clara, and looked back at him. "You want to stay on at the cottage?" she asked, in a voice of wonder.

"If you have no objection. Of course if you want to try to sell, we'll be glad to meet your wishes."

"Sell!" Mrs. Groby stood with her prominent eyes fixed incredulously on him. Her yellow curls and her bright make-up were even more artificial in effect than they were meant to be, against the sick pallor of her skin and the shiny black of her mourning. She said: "We couldn't sell. I was afraid you'd want to go, and that there'd be some mix-up about the rent."

"Not at all. Why should we go? My wife doesn't mind staying there with me, and I hope our friends will turn up, too. I understand that you have inherited Miss Radford's whole estate; let me congratulate you."

"I don't know if we're to be congratulated." Mrs. Groby looked suddenly desolate. "My husband and I are half crazy with all the business involved."

"Settling an estate is always a nuisance. Do you want anything more out of the cottage?"

"Anything more?"

"I believe the sheriff, or somebody, had stuff carted out of the attic."

"Oh; yes. Some old things." Mrs. Groby bit her lip.

"Because if you were willing to leave that nice old furniture, I might consider making you an offer for the place. I couldn't pay anything fancy, you know."

Mrs. Groby rocked on her high heels. After a moment of stupor she asked in a feeble voice: "You want to *buy*?"

"I might consider buying, if this mystery can be cleared up."

"We'd certainly like to sell; we have this farm on our hands, too; we don't want to live out here, especially with the car situation the way it is."

"We wouldn't care to buy it with this mystery hanging over it."

"It's just as much of a mystery to us as it is to you. I don't know what happened. Mr. Gamadge—does Mrs. Gamadge stick to it that she wasn't asleep that night?"

"She sticks to it."

"Well, then, it was autosuggestion; that's what it was! I'm going to have somebody get up and say so at the inquest."

"Autosuggestion?"

"I've read about it. They say you can even make spots come out on yourself, and somebody strangled himself to death once."

"Well; Miss Radford's neck was broken, you know."

Mrs. Groby clutched at her own neck, and rolled her eyes. "Yes, but perhaps they can even do that."

"But why should your aunt victimize herself in such a way? How could she have got into such a state of mind?"

"Haven't you—haven't you heard what they're saying?"

"That Miss Radford poisoned Mrs. Hickson, and was being haunted? We couldn't live in a haunted cottage, Mrs. Groby; my wife's nerves wouldn't stand it; and surely you don't like the idea? Murder in the family?"

"No, but I thought you meant you wouldn't buy the cottage if people thought Mrs. Gamadge—thought Mrs. Gamadge didn't know what did go on that night."

Gamadge looked at her thoughtfully. After a while he said: "I have no anxiety on that score, Mrs. Groby; what I want is to lay the ghost. You know how you can do that, once for all."

"I can?"

"Of course. By authorizing the sheriff to have Mrs. Hickson's body exhumed."

Mrs. Groby again tottered, but recovered her balance to ask eagerly: "And if they didn't find any arsenic, then there wouldn't be any reason for Aunt Eva Hickson to haunt the cottage?"

"Exactly."

Mrs. Groby furiously chewed her lip. "You'd buy the cottage if I could get rid of the ghost idea?"

"Unless you do, we shan't be able to keep servants."

"I'll talk to Mr. Duckett today, soon as I get back to Avebury."

"Good."

They shook hands. Gamadge left her staring into space, and got back into the car. As they drove up the hill towards the Hunters' ridge, he said: "I'm to buy the cottage if Mrs. Hickson's remains contain no arsenic."

"Mrs. Hickson's... But Henry; can we afford to buy the cottage?"

He glanced at her. "We can afford anything, if it results in getting the Grobys on our side and keeping them there."

Before lunch Gamadge took the Hunters aside and told them that he proposed to take his family back to the cottage that afternoon. Hunter looked disappointed, and Fanny almost wept. "I was looking forward to the fun we were going to have," she protested. "And Maggie's a godsend!"

"But Clara's a liability," said Gamadge. "Hunter realizes it, even if you don't, my dear girl."

Hunter said: "You needn't consider that, Gamadge."

"Not consider it? Wait until the inquest! You'd have not only Avebury and Stratfield on your doorstep, you'd have the press of four states and half the cranks in Connecticut. This is a murder."

"It's cruel of you," mourned Fanny, "to take Clara back to that awful place! You weren't there that night; Clara will lose her mind. She was so weak on Sunday that her legs wouldn't hold her up!"

"If she doesn't go back now, her legs may be weak all her life. She may dream periodically of women in sunbonnets, unless I can clear the whole thing away. And what I propose to do," said Gamadge, his eyes on the floor and his hands hanging between his knees, "is to clear it away before she can get up on that witness stand and swear that the woman never came into the bedroom, and that she herself never lost consciousness. If I'm to do that, or even try to do it, I must keep my own hours. I shouldn't be even tolerable as a guest."

Hunter said: "Clara fainted, of course. There's no way out of it. Why the devil can't one keep one's head in a crisis? If I'd kept mine I should have looked at my own watch. I didn't, until Clara asked the time; it was then thirteen minutes to one."

"So Clara tells me."

"And Fanny heard me say so, and Maggie heard me, and I had Duckett on the wire five minutes later. Less. Clara simply must have read the time wrong when she looked at her own watch, or dreamed that she looked at it. I've dreamed—why, I've dreamed that I woke up and looked at my watch, I don't know how often."

"So have I; but we knew afterwards that we did dream it."

"I was half in a dream myself when I heard Clara screaming, and rolled off that bed and out through the living room. And then I looked over Clara's head and saw that door yawning open on space, and saw the poor woman's head on the pillow; I knew her neck was broken before I ever went up to the bed. Of course Clara had seen it too, and her mind went blank; she simply doesn't remember."

"I won't advise her to change her story; if she thinks it's the truth, it will sound like truth on the witness stand; at least, it will sound as if she thought it was true."

"That's a counsel of perfection, but I dare say you're right. Let her tell it as she remembers it, and let them make what they can of it. Clara admits to about half a minute of semi-oblivion, doesn't she?"

"Yes."

"That will have to be enough for them, and I'm not sure that it isn't enough; it wouldn't take longer for a pair of strong hands to break an old woman's neck." Fanny moaned, and Hunter looked at her in self-reproach. "Forgive me, my child."

Gamadge said: "Clara won't admit that the woman could have come into the room at all, much less come up to the bed and killed her patient."

"Oh, Henry," wailed Fanny Hunter, "what are you going to *do*?"

Gamadge lifted his head to smile at her. "Go back to the cottage."

"I couldn't, I never could! I mean, to sleep there!"

Hunter said: "My dear, whatever there was, there was no ghost."

"I'm happy to hear you say so," said Gamadge, still faintly smiling. "I am not sure that a certain member of the state police, and our friend Mrs. Groby, would agree with you."

"Metaphysic, I hope," replied Hunter, "still calls for aid on Sense."

"With you they wouldn't be likely to turn giddy, rave, and die."

Refreshed slightly by this excursion into Pope, Gamadge and Hunter looked smug. Mrs. Hunter said: "I wish I knew what you were talking about."

"About dunces," said Hunter, laughing.

"I only hope that the sheriff of Avebury isn't a dunce; somehow, he doesn't sound like one." Gamadge rose. "Fanny, may I telephone?"

"Of course."

Gamadge made two appointments for the afternoon, and one for the next day. When he came back to the study Fanny was at the hall door. She joined them, to remark that that was Gil Craye.

"He wouldn't come in. He just wanted to leave me some songs to go over. He simply can't believe, Henry, that you're taking Clara back to the cottage!"

"Nobody can believe it."

9

Faded Purple

Gamadge took his car soon after lunch and drove away from the Hunters' farm. Mountain Ridge Road circled the top of the mountain in a rough arc, meeting the route from Avebury at a point midway between that town and a village called Stormer. He drove the four miles to the Radford farm without passing more than two small dwellings and an icehouse; dense woodland was on his left, rolling meadows on his right.

He passed the culvert above the stream, the Radford farm, the branch to the cottage, and Mrs. Simms' place; after that he saw no more houses for three miles, but then came the scattered fringes of Avebury township. He stopped the car when he saw the top of a funerary monument showing to the left above a knoll.

Getting out, he walked up a grass-grown track to the top of the knoll, and looked down at a small old graveyard. A strip of pasture separated it from the woods beyond, and the track he had followed continued past the cemetery, across the field, and up to these woods; no doubt it became the trail that could be seen on the slope behind the cottage.

An ornamental iron fence enclosed the burying ground; he went down and through an arched gateway into a half-acre of old tombstones and graves. It was well cared for, although growth of moss and lichen had been allowed to blacken the half-obliterated names of early settlers. He saw a minatory *Pause, Stranger!*, and an uncompromising *. . . meet thy maker,* before he arrived at milder epitaphs on more modern erections of marble or granite. There was a handsome obelisk, dominating a large enclosed plot, which bore the name in block letters; but the plot contained few graves; the Radfords had been a small or a scattered clan.

In front of the obelisk two graves, side by side, contained the mortal remains of Ephraim (1841–1922) and his wife Evelina. To the right of Evelina lay Eva Radford Hickson, 1878–1941, *At Peace*. To the left of Ephraim the short grass had been marked off into an oblong with pegs and cord; here Alvira would rest.

There was a grave in a corner with a small stone which commemorated one Rhoda Radford, with a date so weather-worn that Gamadge could only suppose Rhoda to have been Ephraim's mother or aunt; and in the opposite corner, under a mountain ash tree, lay John Radford, only son of Ephraim and Evelina, and his wife May. Mrs. Groby's parents; and there was plenty of room for her, and for Groby too.

Gamadge sat on top of John's plain headstone, while grasshoppers whirred about him and the sun beat on his head through the branches of the mountain ash. Eva Hickson had a handsomer monument, a fine granite slab; Gamadge wondered whether the Grobys would put up anything so expensive to Alvira.

He thought it not unbecoming to smoke a cigarette in these precincts. Then he returned to his car, and drove to a large filling station and garage on the outskirts of Avebury. It had once been a thriving concern, with a refreshment counter and all modern conveniences for travelers; but it had lately been permitted to run down. Its counters were bare, its plate glass dim, and there seemed to be only one man on the premises, a sour and sharp-faced youth.

Gamadge asked him to inflate a rear tire. Sitting on a bench while the operation was carried out, he opened a conversation:

"Boss around?"

"No, he ain't."

"Is he up at Radford's, do you know? I see his wife came into that property."

"He ain't there now; he's gone the other way—to trade back a new car—or try to." The young man's sceptical features showed amusement of the cynic's own special kind.

"Quite some trouble up there, I understand," continued Gamadge. "Miss Radford was killed in a cottage she owned, wasn't she?"

"Summer folks got to brawling, and she got in the way."

"Oh. Is that the story?"

"There's plenty of stories; that's Groby's."

Gamadge sat in silence until the tire was ready. Then, after paying the garageman, he said casually: "You might give Mr. Groby a message from me when he gets back. My name's Gamadge. Tell him to call up his wife before he spreads that story of his about Miss Radford's death; he may want to alter it."

He left the young man looking less sceptical now, and more human in his startled interest. Then he drove into town, inquired his way to Dr. Knapp's, and was quickly directed to a frame house on a pleasant street. He rang at the office door, and was admitted by Knapp himself. A minute later they were contemplating each other across the desk in Knapp's office-study. Knapp looked worried and concerned.

"It's a mean thing to happen to you, Mr. Gamadge," said the doctor. "Not much of a home coming. But I'm glad you got here as soon as you did; a nicer young lady than your wife I never met."

"She hasn't made it easy for her friends to do much for her, Doctor; I realize that."

"I'd be glad to do anything I conscientiously could. I can say people faint and don't know they fainted, and I can say it doesn't take more than a second or two for a strong-fingered person to break an old woman's neck; not if they know how, and this person knew how. Hand at the base of the skull, the other hand forcing the chin back. Regular expert."

"So I understand."

"I got out to the cottage at a quarter to two, and I gave it as my best opinion then and later that Alvira had been dead about an hour—about an hour," repeated Knapp. "It's only an opinion. Nothing to go by; no stomach content. When she had her accident Alvira hadn't eaten supper, and I only let them give her liquids afterwards, on account of the shock she had. The autopsy won't place the time of death."

Gamadge, looking at him with something like affection, remarked that it would do no good for Dr. Knapp to stretch the time, kind as it was of him to suggest doing so. "My wife says that when she began her watch Alvira Radford was breathing audibly."

"I thought perhaps the woman might have got in while Mrs. Hunter was doing her spell; Mrs. Hunter didn't sit in the bedroom, you know. Somebody might have managed it sometime between eleven and twelve."

"We won't ask you to get up and say all that on oath, Doctor."

"I'd be willing—it's only a medical opinion either way. The lampshade was tilted, and Mrs. Gamadge says she never once looked at the bed after she saw that door open. Darnedest story I ever listened to."

"It is. Would you be willing to tell me something about Mrs. Hickson's death, Doctor?"

Knapp started violently. "Eva Hickson's, did you say?"

"Yes. You looked after her, didn't you? Did you think she was going to die so soon?"

Knapp suddenly looked angry. "Nothing in that story, not a thing; it's these darned gabbling country neighbors. There never was any question about Eva Hickson's death; she could have died of several natural causes, but I diagnosed collapse after flu, intestinal flu. It may have been gastroenteritis. I wasn't called in till she was pretty low with it, saw her twice in the week before she went. She didn't like doctors; nearly died of blood poisoning one summer because she wouldn't have an infected hand seen to. Paid her bills, you know, but hated to run 'em up."

"You weren't surprised, then, when Hawley got hold of you that Sunday afternoon and told you she was dead?"

"Surprised? Woman of over sixty, in her weakened condition and with her symptoms? No. No doctor would have been surprised. Naturally I gave the certificate. As for the gossip afterwards, *you'd* be surprised at the ignorance of these country people even now; they don't know a thing about disease, and they like excitement. If a person dies, the doctor gave 'em the wrong medicine, or the relatives neglected 'em. If the patient had money, she—or he—was murdered for it. I heard the talk, but I knew it would die down."

"Had Miss Radford heard it, do you know?"

"If she had, she didn't mention it to me."

"I can take it, then, that you never at any time suspected arsenic?"

Knapp uncrossed his short legs, recrossed them, and threw himself pettishly about in his chair. "When the talk began, of course I went over the case in my mind. Eva Hickson complained of her legs, but she always complained of 'em; she had arthritis. Perhaps I didn't listen very hard when she talked about her legs; no doctor listens very hard to old symptoms of that kind when he's trying to cure something else."

"Did Alvira ever tell you why she put up that fence of hers, and bought those Baskerville hounds?"

"I haven't seen her to speak to since Eva Hickson's death; I mean I hadn't, till Saturday night."

"Well, Doctor." Gamadge rose and held out his hand. "I'm definitely obliged to you for your interest, and for what you were willing to do for us."

"Never met a nicer girl than your wife."

"I'm afraid she'll have a bad time of it at the inquest unless they can make sense of her testimony. I'm working on it. I hope, by the way, Doctor, that you'll consider yourself our family physician while we're at the cottage."

Knapp stood beside his desk, staring at Gamadge. He repeated in a disbelieving tone: "At the cottage?"

"Yes. We're moving in this afternoon, I hope."

"Mrs. Gamadge had a shock—a bad shock there. Is it wise?"

"She says she's willing to go back."

Knapp continued to stare. Gamadge said, smiling, "Do you know something, Doctor? I believe you think there may have been arsenic in Mrs. Hickson's medicine after all."

Knapp said nothing.

"And that there may have been a ghost at the cottage on Saturday night."

"Pshah."

But he said no more; he shook hands silently, and silently accompanied Gamadge to the side door.

Gamadge found Avebury Town Hall with no difficulty, and climbed the stairs to Duckett's office on the stroke of three. Duckett and young Mr. Ledwell of Stratfield were also on time for the appointment; Duckett, an imperturbable man of fifty-odd with a bald head and a sorrel moustache, shook hands with Gamadge and then resumed his swivel chair. He did not seem anxious to direct proceedings or to talk at all, but tilted the chair back and continued to chew. His manner was detached.

Mr. Ledwell shook Gamadge's hand with a certain firmness; he looked very keen, and if he had a tight mouth and a narrow eye, he also had a well-shaped head, a strong chin and a straight back. His expression implied that he expected a certain amount of truculence in Mrs. Gamadge's husband, but he was disappointed. Gamadge was blandness itself.

"Thanks very much for coming over and saving me the trip to Stratfield, Mr. Ledwell. Not that I should have minded going, but time is important to us all in this case."

"I can't discuss the case with you at all, Mr. Gamadge; not at the present stage of it. I can only listen to your comments, and to any new evidence your wife may have for us. I hope she has new evidence—something she forgot to mention before."

"Nothing new, Mr. Ledwell."

Ledwell sat down, and Gamadge took the only remaining chair, which faced the sun. He did not turn it away from the window, but allowed the full glare of the western light to fall upon his blunt features and amiable smile. "I didn't come to discuss the case, either," he said. "I came to ask you and the sheriff whether my wife and I may move into the cottage this afternoon. And our cook, of course."

Mr. Ledwell's eyes widened; Sheriff Duckett's remained half closed, and he chewed calmly on.

"We are now," continued Gamadge, "as everybody knows, staying at Mountain Ridge Farm with Mr. and Mrs. Phineas Hunter. But we can't further impose on them; we must go elsewhere. Not far, since it would not be convenient to you to have Mrs. Gamadge too far away until after the inquest. The cottage is the logical place, I think; after all, we're paying for it. Will you or somebody arrange matters with the state police?"

Ledwell said after a pause: "I must say, Mr. Gamadge, that I'm very much surprised at your wife's being willing to go back to the cottage after her experience there."

"I shall be with her this time; and although she was in the room where Miss Radford was murdered, and saw the murderer, she didn't see the murder. By the way—do you think there *was* a woman in a sunbonnet, or do you think it was a ghost—Mrs. Hickson's ghost?"

The sheriff moved slightly, and hooked his thumbs into his suspenders; Ledwell said in an angry tone: "Ghost? Ghosts do not break peoples' necks, Mr. Gamadge!"

"I ask because so many people do seem to think it was a ghost. My servant of course does, my wife did, Mrs. Groby does, Mrs. Hunter does, Mrs. Simms and her hired man probably do, and though Knapp will deny it for the honor of science, I think he does himself. After all, immense trouble was taken to persuade people to believe in a ghost; the whole masquerade, lasting for more than a week, was carried out to that end. You know some of the evidence that was presented to my wife; the murderer's dress and sunbonnet, which my wife knows were of the same material as the dress and the sunbonnet, Mrs. Hickson's property, which you found in the attic."

Ledwell glanced at the sheriff, turned back to Gamadge, placed an elbow on the desk, and extended a forefinger: "Your wife did not inform us that she had seen those garments in the attic wardrobe, Mr. Gamadge."

"Nor have you asked her to look at them, and identify them with the garments she described as worn by the murderer. No doubt they will be sprung on her at the inquest; but why wait until then?"

Ledwell said sharply: "I am not obliged to acquaint

witnesses with what evidence I may possess, Mr. Gamadge."

"But why not try to find out what evidence there is, unless you are building up a special case?"

"I am not trying to build up a case."

"But I am. I know that a human being, impelled by some motive at present unknown, murdered Alvira Radford. That person came to the bedroom door on Saturday night or Sunday morning, and pushed the plug from the keyhole; my wife heard it fall, and you learned of it from her, although she did not at that time understand the significance of the sound. The lock was turned by means of one of the house keys. The door had never been sealed, and was pushed open. As for those purple garments, anyone could visit the attic without being seen by my wife or by Maggie, as you must have discovered for yourselves. There is nothing supernatural about these facts, and the circumstances of the murder itself, however incomprehensible it may at present seem, are not supernatural either.

"That is my view of the case so far; but it is not yours."

The sheriff turned a lacklustre eye on Gamadge. Ledwell, flushing darkly, said: "I do not propose to tell you what my views are, Mr. Gamadge."

"I will tell you what they are. You have followed the line of least resistance. You ignore the plug from the keyhole, which is evidence that somebody came through that door, and you say what my wife feared that you would say unless she withheld the fact that she had seen the purple dress and sunbonnet in the attic: that she had had a hallucination, based on the woman in the sunbonnet whom she and Maggie had seen about the cottage, the clothes in the attic, and the gossip about Mrs. Hickson's death by poison."

Duckett had stopped chewing; Ledwell was silent.

"But you go farther than that," continued Gamadge. "You tell yourself that my wife was so worked upon by these matters, that Miss Radford's accident was a last straw; you tell yourself that during the night of the murder she temporarily lost her reason; that she identified herself with the avenging ghost of Eva Hickson, built up the scene she afterwards described from figments supplied by her own imagination, and herself killed Alvira Radford in a fit of homicidal mania. That is what will be suggested at the inquest, on her own evidence; and if she doesn't realize it herself, it's because she is too sane to entertain a possibility so absurd."

When Ledwell at last spoke it was in a tone of regret: "I can only say that it's a theory, Mr. Gamadge, and that in default of any other we must of course consider it."

"And I have considered how to deal with it. I can assure you without prejudice that it's impossible—not in her inheritance, her history, or her mental make-up; but that assurance will carry little weight with you. I propose to do what I can to supply you with another, and I can work best from the cottage."

Ledwell said, rather awkwardly, that there could be no objection to his taking Mrs. Gamadge back to the cottage if he saw none himself.

"She didn't go mad there before, if that's what you mean, and I can promise you that she won't go mad there now."

Duckett spoke for the first time: "I have that plug that came out of the keyhole, Mr. Gamadge; I looked around for it as soon as your wife told me she heard something drop on the floor. I don't suppose I would have looked, or it would never have been found, if she hadn't mentioned it; it's like a splinter off the woodwork, and it was off in a corner under the edge of the mat.

"I found out that the front-door keys fit that back-door lock; but when I looked they were both in their own doors. I've combed the county for prowlers, Mr. Gamadge; can't place one in that vicinity at the times specified by Mrs. Gamadge and your help.

"I had a kind of theory myself, for a while. The bed was right under the window. I thought the window screen might have been moved, and Alvira Radford killed from outside the cottage. But those screens fit tight, and if your wife was asleep the noise would have woke her up."

"I know, Sheriff; I thought of the window myself." Gamadge took out his cigarette case, lighted a cigarette, and smoked for some time in silence. Then he said: "I know it's a problem. I'll be quite frank with you; I'm out first of all to demolish the avenging ghost theory. The murderer built up evidence for it in order to localize the murder—keep peoples' minds on the Radford sisters and the cottage, on the possibility of an old crime. If that's what the murderer wants, we must do the other thing; get rid of the ambiguous and the spectral, and bring the facts of the matter out into the open. One fact above all—that there was a flesh-and-blood murderer, with a motive. There's only one way to make it definite; by exhuming Mrs. Hickson. If she wasn't poisoned by Alvira Radford, there was no reason for her to come back and kill Alvira to prevent Alvira from putting flowers on her grave."

Duckett ceased to chew, but he said nothing. Ledwell spoke frowningly: "Exhumation is a serious matter."

"Mrs. Groby is willing to have it done."

"She is?" Ledwell stared. "Most people don't care for the publicity."

Duckett said: "There needn't be any. I could get it done at night."

"Before the inquest?" Gamadge looked at him.

"Right away."

"Thanks. And I'd be very grateful to you if you'd tell me exactly how much money Mrs. Hickson left to Miss Radford."

"A hundred and six thousand and sixty-four dollars and seven cents," said Duckett, "but the taxes cut into it."

"Thanks. And I'd like to see that dress and that sunbonnet you found in the attic."

Ledwell frowned more heavily. "I only want the truth of this matter," he said, "but those garments will probably be state's evidence; if we have a trial, you know. I don't feel justified..."

Duckett tilted his chair forward, put his elbows on his desk, and addressed the state's attorney in his dispassionate drawl:

"Ledwell, this feller's in trouble. He comes home from overseas and finds his summer plans all upset and his wife mixed up in a homicide. His wife's as nice a woman as ever I met. She don't holler or complain, she sees us all, she don't make up stories about being in a faint or asleep, which is all she'd have to do to get out of the business now and hereafter. I say give these folks a chance. I can get a court order and have that exhumation done tomorrow night; I can get the inquest put off till we have the report from the Hartford laboratory. I'm willin' Mr. Gamadge should see the things, if he thinks they may help him to solve the case."

Gamadge thought that the two exchanged a very odd look; but he said: "I'm extremely grateful."

Duckett rose, went into an inner room, and came back with a large, loosely wrapped paper package. This he opened, disclosing a bundle of faded calico, purple, with a pattern of small black sprigs. The dress had been turned on itself twice lengthwise, and the sunbonnet wrapped inside it; he laid both out flat on the desk top. Then he straightened, and looked at Gamadge.

His expression was no more peculiar than Gamadge's own, and Ledwell watched them both with bright, sharp eyes.

Presently Gamadge leaned forward, took a bit of the material between thumb and finger, and after a moment put it down again. He questioned the sheriff incredulously: "Are these—just as you took them out of that wardrobe in the attic?"

"Just." He added: "Ever since I saw them I've been teetering on the edge of the ghost theory myself."

"I don't blame you."

"I was out there that night; I saw Alvira Radford on that bed, and I saw that door swingin'; and then later I found these things hangin' up in that attic, among all Eva Hickson's junk." He pointed a long, knotty finger at the relics on the desk. "I took 'em off the hook myself. Those creases in that dress haven't been shook out for months, I should say; and nobody untied those sunbonnet strings four days ago. Nobody untied 'em months ago. Look at the knot."

Gamadge looked; he seemed unable to cease looking.

"They've hung there, on a bet," said Duckett, "since Eva Hickson wore 'em; early last summer, perhaps. Nobody wore 'em to scare Mrs. Gamadge with, or to scare anybody with; or to kill Alvira Radford in. That's why I'm teetering on the edge of the ghost theory, and that's why Ledwell thinks Mrs. Gamadge was seeing things; it's just as well, Mr. Gamadge, for you to know what you're up against."

Gamadge raised his eyes to Ledwell. "I know what I'm up against," he said. "I must get busy. Thank you both."

"Thank us for nothing." Duckett, looking pessimistic, began to wrap up the purple dress. He avoided touching it or the sunbonnet, and he eyed them with disgust.

"For something," Gamadge told him, straightening and smiling. "For letting me know what I have to prove; that Mrs. Hickson had two dresses and two sunbonnets, just alike."

He shook hands, saluted them both gaily, and went out.
"Who is he, anyway?" Ledwell gazed after him.

"I don't know. But the gov'ment sent him abroad," said
Duckett, "so perhaps he's as smart anyway as we are."

10

Foreign Bodies

In her anxiety to fall in with Gamadge's plans, Clara had
suppressed her doubts and fears; but when the time came
to return to the cottage she found to her amazement that
she was not only resigned to the move, but looking
forward to it. Gamadge's high spirits and Maggie's compla-
cency carried her along, and the move itself was an easy
one. Maggie, ensconced in the rumble of the Gamadge
car, with a lump of ice done up in newspaper at her feet
and half a cooked ham in her arms, said that there would
be no ghosts with Mr. Gamadge in the house. Gamadge
talked with almost febrile intensity of his yearning for dips
in the pool and walks in the woods.

"I want to hear the waterfall," he kept saying, in the
tones of a minor poet crazed by inspiration. "I want to
hear the waterfall."

Clara wanted to hear the waterfall, too.

They stopped at the Radford farm. Sam the hired man
said that he guessed they could go on having dairy produce,
and forthwith supplied them with a can of milk and a
pound of butter. He promised eggs for the morrow.

"What became of the dogs?" asked Gamadge.

"They was drafted into the Coast Guard."

"Where did Miss Radford get them, do you know?"

"Kennels over the mountain near Stormer. She went
there on and off for three weeks after she got settled in
here, makin' herself acquainted with them; then when
they came she introdooced them to me."

"On formal terms, were you?"

"Kind of. They let me give them their supper and wash
'em up sometimes. With Alvira lookin' on."

"Mrs. Groby here?"

"No, she goes home by sunset. Certainly gettin' the old house turned inside out."

"That's what heirs are for."

At the cottage Eli the Indian was waiting on the porch. He said that he had taken over after the state trooper left, just to see that everything was in good shape when the Gamadges came. He had a bunch of flowers for Clara, picked in his own garden; his shack was two miles away in the heart of the reservation.

Clara pored lovingly over the sweet williams, marigolds and mourning bride. "Eli, it was nice of you."

Eli, grave and calm, said that he had an idee Mrs. Gamadge liked flowers. Gamadge offered him a cigarette, and they sat smoking while Clara got out vases and her clipping scissors.

"Are you inclined to the ghost theory, Eli?" inquired Gamadge. "Do you think my wife saw a ghost on Saturday night?"

Eli said: "Tell you what, Mr. Gamadge; when I give up being a ward of the government so I could vote, I must have given up ghosts too. I don't seem to think much of 'em now, if I ever did."

"I don't believe she saw a ghost, either."

"There weren't no tracks around the place, nothing the law and the newspaper fellers and the sightseers couldn't have left. The grass and the leaves—you don't get footprints on 'em. You want me to help fix anything before I go?"

Gamadge produced a brown paper package. When opened it disclosed a new brass bolt, four screws, and a screw driver. "I thought I'd just put this on the back door, and take down the bed."

He and Eli screwed the bolt on, took the bed down, and carried bed and bedding up to the empty attic. Then, since Eli said that they might as well finish the chore, they moved out the rest of the furniture—dresser, night table and chairs. It was light stuff, and they got it up into the attic too. Clara, much pleased, hung all the family raincoats and outer wraps in the curtained recess across a corner of the little room, and said that now they had a decent entry, and how cool it would make the house.

"We'll have to get a screen for the door," said Gamadge.

Eli remarked that he believed he had seen one in the barn; and indeed there proved to be one which had undoubtedly belonged in that entrance. They screwed it up with hardware which Eli found at the bottom of one of his leather pockets.

"You'll have to do a better job on it sometime," he said, "but it'll keep out the bugs for now."

Gamadge forced a bill on him; he went off, smiling his antique smile.

Gamadge had his first dip in the pool under the waterfall, and then Clara called him to supper. Afterwards they sat out on the porch drinking their coffee.

"You're a sport not to do me out of this," he said. "I know it was tough for you to come back."

"I haven't minded it for one single minute, and since you made that bedroom disappear the cottage is like new. It's just *gone*," said Clara. "It's as though nothing ever happened in it; it isn't a room, even, any more."

"Maggie will like our being able to stack our wet bathing things and umbrellas there. This weather won't hold forever, I suppose."

"We can be cosy when it rains."

"Can't we, though?" He added: "Hello, more company."

The state trooper rode up on his motorcycle. He said, balanced at the foot of the path, "You really got here."

"All settled, too. Come up and have some coffee," said Gamadge. "And you can lay a bet, too; if you want to lose it."

"Bet?" The trooper, one eye on Clara, drank coffee standing.

"That you can't find the little green bedroom."

"The—the murder room?"

"It's vanished. There's something wrong with this cottage, officer."

The trooper squinted at him, set his cup down, and went unceremoniously into the house. When he came out he was smiling. "Certainly makes a difference."

"We think so."

"I kind of had Mrs. Gamadge on my mind, but I guess she'll be all right with the boy friend."

Clara, wincing, said that she would.

"And he'll persuade you you went off into a doze that night."

"I'm tackling the problem from a different angle," said Gamadge.

"You are?"

"Of course I am."

"Well, I certainly am glad you have one. I didn't like the idea of Mrs. Gamadge gettin' up at the inquest and tellin' the ghost story."

"Very strange story, but true."

The officer looked at him, finished his coffee in silence, and then said good night and rode away. Clara said: "Does he believe in the ghost, Henry?"

"He doesn't know what to believe. Now I'll tax *your* credulity some more; that woman in the sunbonnet wasn't wearing the things you saw in the attic, Clara."

"She *wasn't?*"

"No. The sheriff showed them to me today, and he and Ledwell know that the woman never wore them. They haven't been out of their creases for a long time, and the strings of the sunbonnet haven't been untied for ages. I don't believe those things have been worn since Mrs. Hickson last wore them, certainly as long ago as early last summer; she died in the first week of July, you know, and she probably wasn't out for two weeks before that—she was ailing."

Clara moved nearer to him. "Then—what did I see?" She added, her voice tremulous, "And who opened the attic door?"

"Somebody who had dressed up in Mrs. Hickson's other set of working clothes. Haven't you ever ordered two sets of things alike?"

"Yes, often; tennis things and wash dresses."

"One for the tub, one to wear. That's what Mrs. Hickson did, but unfortunately we have no one to tell us what her habits were, unless her friends in Stratfield can—those dressmakers, you know. The purple clothes were hand-hemmed and finished; they never came from a factory. I only hope Mrs. Hickson or Miss Radford didn't make them. I can ask Mrs. Groby whether there's a sewing machine at the farm."

Clara insisted: "Henry, why was the attic door opened, if nobody wanted to get the purple things out of it?"

"To make your flesh creep. To convince you, and through you others, that the murder was strictly in the family; and that's what did convince you—the trick worked."

He called Mrs. Groby on the telephone. She told him that she had spoken to Duckett, and that there was no sewing machine at the farm.

"They've started badgering us about alibis, Mr. Gamadge," she went on, in a quavering voice. "Walt's nearly crazy. Who has any alibis for the middle of the night, except a person's wife or husband?"

"Nobody in Avebury, I should hope. They have to do it, Mrs. Groby."

"But what's the use? I wouldn't tell if Walt had been out till morning, which he often is, with a garage business and everything." She faltered: "They're just badgering him to death."

"They have to; you got all the money, you know."

Mrs. Groby gave a kind of screeching wail, and rang off. Gamadge returned to Clara, looking interested. "No sewing machine, and, unless I'm greatly mistaken, no money."

"No *money?*"

"Mrs. Groby is agitated, and not only because Mr. Groby is being investigated ruthlessly." He took his wife's hand. "Listen to that waterfall."

"It's very gentle tonight; the stream must be getting low."

"If it weren't for you I shouldn't be hearing it at all."

The weather still held next day. Gamadge took Clara with him to Stratfield, but when they reached the village he left her and the car in front of the public library. Then, having been told by a man in a drugstore how to find the old Craye mansion, he walked along the main street to the next corner, and turned left.

Stratfield, except for its small and inconspicuous business section, was an eighteenth-century county seat of memorable beauty. It was set rather high, between the river and a mountain, miles from any railroad, and its churches, courthouse and original dwellings had been religiously preserved from restoration. At least, their outsides were as they had always been; the Craye mansion, shaded by its maples and surrounded by its acres of lawn, must have looked very much as it did now when imported English workmen finished slating its roof before the Revolution.

But a faint green patina was now to be seen on the gravel of the drive, and the hedge required clipping.

Gamadge was observing these by-products of war (if such they were) when Gilbert Craye cantered up on a brown pony, dismounted, and shook hands. They walked on to the house together, Craye with the pony's rein over his arm.

"Perfectly lovely place," said Gamadge.

"You'll find it a trifle crowded, at present; with my refugees, you know."

"I didn't know."

"Didn't you? We all take them so much for granted now that nobody thinks to mention them, I suppose. I've had refugees," said Craye, switching the unclipped hedge with his riding crop, "for a couple of years."

"Who are they?"

"This lot? Don't ask me. People push them on me, and I ask no questions. I ought to do what I can, you know, since I'm disqualified for service. It wasn't so bad when I had my staff, but now, oh Lord."

"You sound as though you had a dozen refugees."

"I have five at present, counting the Medos children. Medos is a Greek, I believe, and one of the women is a German, old Bavarian family, and one's English; married to a Frenchman, poor devil, but she hasn't heard from him for a long time now."

"What a combination; do they enjoy each other's society?"

"I don't think they foregather much. How's Mrs. Gamadge?"

"Splendid. We moved to the cottage yesterday."

Craye stopped short, and the pony threw up its head. "You did?"

"Why not?"

"Well . . ." They moved on again. "She went through a pretty grim experience there."

"Clara doesn't find it grim now."

"Grim story, though. Who did strangle the old lady? Does anybody know yet?"

"I have no information; but a good many of the natives seem to think that Mrs. Hickson strangled her; or rather, broke her neck."

Again Craye stopped, and again the pony backed and skittered nervously. "Mrs. Hickson? You mean the dead sister?"

"Because Miss Radford poisoned her; so they suspect."

"Mrs. Gamadge said something. I never heard of such a thing."

"Very sensational."

They walked on, and Craye began to whistle. Gamadge said: "So they're going to exhume Mrs. Hickson and find out."

Craye stopped whistling. "Find out?"

"Whether they can't eliminate Mrs. Hickson's ghost as a suspect. No crime last summer, no ghost this summer. I want the ghost eliminated, of course, because I want attention focused on the party who impersonated the ghost and committed the murder."

"You care?"

"Yes. Ledwell wants Clara to take the rap for the murder; as a dangerous intermittent maniac, you know." Gamadge spoke without emphasis. Craye, this time apparently quite staggered, stood looking at him with every freckle standing out on his fair skin.

He said: "Ledwell's crazy himself."

"Well, no. What would you or I think if we read about this murder in the papers? But I don't want Clara in the papers, held for examination, for all I know railroaded to an asylum for the criminal insane."

"Good Lord, Gamadge, you exaggerate! It would never come to that."

"In my place, would you want it to come to anything? I have the weekend to find out who did wear that sunbonnet, and why Miss Alvira Radford was killed. In order to get anywhere I must find out something about Miss Radford."

They had arrived at the noble portico, with its fluted columns and its grave pediment. A youth came around the corner of the house and took the pony. Craye turned the knob of the white door, muttered irritably, and plied the knocker; the door was opened almost immediately by a pale, slender woman in a blue dress. Her hair was so light a gold as to be almost silvery; her features resembled those once seen in the old gift annuals; she had the wide forehead, large eyes, oval cheeks and small mouth, she had even the sloping shoulders and the long, slim waist of the Keepsakes.

"Thank you, Mrs. Star," said Craye, as they passed her. She bowed without smiling, and closed the door after them. Then she turned, and went into a room on the left.

"That cuts out the library," said Craye. "I didn't introduce you, because when she's on these premises Mrs. Star likes to pretend that she's a domestic. Her idea of working out her board, I think."

"She is the German lady?" Gamadge's eyes were on two children who sat close together halfway up the broad stairs; they were very small, of indeterminate sex, sharp-chinned and pale; with thick dark hair and great black eyes. They sat silent, staring back at him.

"Yes." Craye looked up at the children and saluted them with his riding crop. "Nearly got us quarantined last month," he muttered to Gamadge. "Came out in spots, but it was only prickly heat, or something repulsive."

He led the way into a room on the right; a large drawing room, stately and high, done up for the summer in flowered chintz. As they entered, a short, dark man rose from a chair beside a window, closed his book, and stood leaning slightly forward and smiling.

"Mr. Medos," said Craye, "Mr. Gamadge."

The dark man bowed, and said in the accents of Oxford, "I am just going."

"Not at all, don't disturb yourself; I'm taking Gamadge into the back parlor," said Craye.

Gamadge was piloted through a double doorway into a kind of study, rich and sombre, where a stocky gray-haired woman sat working at a jigsaw puzzle. She said "Ow," and made as if to rise.

"All right, Madame Fouret, don't get up." Craye hustled Gamadge towards a door on the left.

"I'm only witing for my cike to bike," said Madame Fouret, smiling.

"I hope you put lots of plums in it." Craye now had Gamadge by the arm, and got him across the back hall and into a manorial dining room. He pulled out an armchair for his guest, one for himself, and sank down with a sigh, only to start up again: "Sherry? Whiskey? Anything?"

"Not a thing. You seem to be pulling your weight, I must say." Gamadge did not suppress his amusement.

"I don't know." Craye laid his riding crop on the table in front of him. "Fouret does a lot of cooking, and makes the Medos kids wash themselves now and then. Medos is writing a book, but he does some accounts for me. Mrs.

Star is trying to get a job; you wouldn't know anybody that wants to learn German?"

"Not at the moment. Beautiful creature she is. Is her real name a secret?"

"Not at all; but she prefers this one."

"I should think she would be useful in half a dozen departments, if she's properly vouched for."

"She doesn't seem to find anything. Never mind my refugees, they're my headache, and sometimes a splitting one. Did you think I could be of any use to you in this business about the Radford murder?"

"Perhaps. As I said, I must find out something about Miss Radford, and from what Clara told me I thought *you* knew something."

"I?"

"Didn't you imply that Miss Radford had been gossiping, or that friends of hers had been gossiping about her, or something of the kind?"

"I don't remember that I did. I hardly knew the woman by sight; if I spoke of her at all, I was probably joking."

"Clara thinks you really had some unfavorable knowledge of Miss Radford."

"I hadn't. Mrs. Gamadge is mistaken. And if I had," said Craye, "it certainly wouldn't be the kind of knowledge to help you out in this case."

Gamadge sat back, looking at him. Craye returned the look with one so unlike his ordinary expression of smiling amiability that he might have been a stranger. It was as a stranger that Gamadge at last addressed him:

"You understand that while Clara's in trouble or danger I can't consider any other person?"

"She's in no danger. She must change her evidence, that's all."

"I like it as it is."

They held each other's eyes. Then Craye, looking down at his clasped hands, said: "I'd help you out if I could."

"Perhaps, then, you'll tell me where to find these friends of the deceased? These dressmakers or sewing women."

Craye, his eyes still lowered, sat without moving while a great clock in the corner told the seconds as they passed. Finally he said: "Name of Jeans, on the right-hand side of the Mill Road after you cross the bridge. Don't believe a word they say."

Gamadge rose. "Thanks; but are you asking that as a favor?"

Craye, flushing, also got to his feet. "I'm saving you time."

"I'm glad you realize that it's precious."

They went in silence to the front door, and in silence Gamadge walked away.

11

Patchwork

When Gamadge returned to the Stratfield Public Library he found Clara where she had promised to be—among the stacks, reading. He looked over her shoulder. "Brushing up on early Henry James, are you?"

"I thought I dimly remembered—" she looked up at him.

"But you found that *The Romance of Certain Old Clothes* isn't really the source of this romance of old clothes, didn't you?"

"I just dimly remembered that there were old clothes, and that somebody got strangled." She closed the book.

"Motive, characters and setting all wrong, aren't they?"

"And the social background is wrong. Our characters are just country people."

"Er—some of them."

She got up to search his face anxiously. "Did Gilbert Craye tell you anything about Miss Radford?"

"He says you're mistaken, that he couldn't have meant what you thought he meant."

"Oh dear, he did, though."

"He will think twice, after this, before he speaks; that is, if he really has more mind than a fly."

"Of course he has more mind than a fly! Phineas Hunter thinks he has no mind because he doesn't read anything."

"Doesn't read Pope," laughed Gamadge.

They returned the book, and went out into the broad sunny street. It did not take them long to leave the charms of Stratfield behind them; the Mill Road, dipping sharply to the river, led to a region of swampy fields and dejected-looking willows. Beyond an old covered bridge there were small and ugly houses, surrounded by thin vegetable gardens and hung about with washing-lines.

"The wrong side of the tracks," said Gamadge, "if Stratfield had tracks. Well, I suppose every town must have its back yard. Here we are."

He stopped in front of a bleak little house, with a sign in a window—handwritten—which said: *Dressmaking*.

"You'd better stay in the car, Clara." Gamadge descended. "We haven't time to discuss your new dress today; we only have time to find out whether they'll make it."

"I'm glad I'm going to have a new dress."

"Hope you'll like it." He went up the path to the open front door, and turned the knob of a bell. It rang harshly, and its summons was answered by a tall, middle-aged woman with a pincushion fastened to the belt of her apron. She looked at him, and past him at Clara and the car. Her expression said that the last thing she expected was a customer. Her angry-looking mouth hardly troubled to smile at this nuisance who was probably asking the way to Hartford.

"What was it?" she demanded.

"Mrs. Jeans?"

"I'm Miss Jeans." She added, in a tone of surprise, "You want to talk to Mother?"

"And to you, if I may. We're from North Avebury; we've rented Miss Radford's cottage for the summer, and from something that was said we understood you did dressmaking."

"You're Alvira Radford's summer tenants?" Her look changed to one of ravenous interest.

"Yes; wasn't it tragic about her death? I didn't come up till afterwards; only got there on Tuesday; but my wife was in the cottage when it happened."

Miss Jeans looked as if she wanted to ask whether he thought she didn't know that. She said instead: "Come in. Ain't your wife getting out of the car?"

"Well, no; she's rather tired. She wanted me to ask whether you could make her a summer dress."

Miss Jeans ushered him into a musty sitting room, where old Mrs. Jeans sat beside a window; she was engaged in sewing narrow strips of parti-colored material end to end, and balls of completed work lay in a basket at her feet. A sewing machine in front of the other window, and an ironing board on trestles, betrayed the fact that the sitting room was also the Jeanses' workroom.

Mrs. Jeans looked up with an expression forbidding in the extreme; it was one of instinctive suspicion, mingled with an all-embracing dislike for her fellow creatures. Miss Jeans rapidly explained Gamadge and his errand; he supplied his name.

Old Mrs. Jeans, curiosity obscuring malignity, invited him to sit down. He did so in a chair pulled forward for him by Miss Jeans, who took up a commanding position behind her mother's chair.

"Alvira Radford recommended us?" asked the old lady.

"We understand that you sewed for her."

"Not much nowadays."

Miss Jeans said: "I do the dressmakin' now, what there is of it. People buy these cheap ready-made things, and wear 'em a couple of months, and throw 'em away. They got to; the material falls to pieces after one wash."

"My wife doesn't like that kind of thing at all," said Gamadge. "She'd supply her own material—just a simple summer dress."

"I guess you men don't know it, but nothing's simple about dressmakin' now," said Miss Jeans, in a lecturing tone. "The priorities make it hard to get findings; pins and needles, hooks and eyes. Thread, even."

"We understand that. My wife would supply findings."

"If she wants quilts or rag rugs," said Mrs. Jeans, "I can make her those—if she gives me time."

"My mother's quilts get prizes at fairs," said Miss Jeans. "I'll tell Mrs. Gamadge."

Old Mrs. Jeans could no longer sacrifice her curiosity even to her business; she asked: "What are they saying about Alvira's death? Do they still think some crazy woman got in?"

"Well, if she did, she wore a sunbonnet."

"A sunbonnet?"

"So my wife says. As a disguise, of course. There aren't so many seen about nowadays, are there? My wife was quite surprised to find one in the attic of the cottage; among some things that belonged, I think, to Miss Radford's sister; a sister who died."

Miss Jeans drew herself up: "I made that sunbonnet!"

"No, really?"

"And the dress that went with it. I made both sets."

"Both sets?"

"Mis' Hickson always got enough material for two dresses. It's cheaper that way," said Miss Jeans, reassuming her patronizing tone. "She got so much that she had me make two sunbonnets."

"I suppose she wore out the other one. My wife liked the pattern, she thought it must have been quite pretty when it was new."

Mrs. Jeans said: "She can see a piece. Belle, did I use all the scraps in that quilt, or are there any more in the bag?"

"I don't know." Miss Jeans went to a walnut chest of drawers, and brought back a folded patchwork quilt, still incompletely quilted. Among squares and triangles of red, blue, yellow and white Gamadge's eye discerned a recurrent rectangle of purple, sprigged with black.

"Nice quilt," he said. "My wife must see it when she comes in."

"I should think she'd be all worn out," said Mrs. Jeans affably, "after that night she had when Alvira was killed. The trouble is, there's a riffraff around everywhere now. We pay taxes, but we don't get protection from prowlers."

"And of course now there are refugees, too," said Gamadge.

"Coming from nobody knows where," agreed Miss Jeans, "and half of 'em probably spies."

"Have you any in Stratfield?"

"There's a half dozen up at Craye's," said old Mrs. Jeans, "if they are refugees. I should say one of 'em isn't; but you couldn't get your nose inside the door to find out; even the authorities couldn't—or wouldn't. It got so bad, certain parties complained to the authorities; but they wouldn't move against Gilbert Craye, he's too rich."

Miss Jeans said: "I went up there to collect junk for our war chest, you can imagine the junk there must be in those attics; or haven't you seen the Craye place?"

"I've seen it; beautiful."

"We make a list," said Miss Jeans, "and then we send a

truck. But that houseman—he's gone now to do defense work—would he let me into the hall, even? He would not. He opened the door a crack, paid no attention when I told him my name, and said it had been attended to; but Gilbert Craye sent no junk to the bazaar."

"I sewed for years up at the Craye mansion," said Mrs. Jeans. "Plain work, slip covers, mending, and old Mrs. Craye's summer wrappers. I used to sit and talk with her for hours, and had my place at the lunch table. I was good enough to sit at lunch with Squire Craye; but that son of his won't see my daughter."

"Inconsiderate," murmured Gamadge. "Still, it's very patriotic of him, or something—having all those refugees."

Miss Jeans and Mrs. Jeans looked at each other. Miss Jeans said: "You ought to see the German."

"Is there a German?"

"Married woman, and can't get a divorce. He's an officer in the German army, and she can't get a divorce!"

"Because her uncle's a cardinal," said Mrs. Jeans. "So the story goes, and I think the minister started it."

"I don't know what the gov'ment is thinking of," said Miss Jeans, "sending a young married woman to live with a young feller like Gilbert Craye. Two young children in the house, too."

"And no older woman?"

"Of course there's an older woman for looks, but you can imagine how much she would have to say—about what Gilbert Craye does and don't do! Why, Alvira Radford saw him and the German as long ago as last summer, way off on the reservation road, and sittin' in the reservation woods. They went as far as North Avebury for their drives. Why, none of us here even knew there was such a woman at the Craye house till Alvira Radford began to talk about the light-haired married woman Gilbert Craye was carrying on with. It don't look good to our allies to have these enemy aliens we have here actin' like that. But the county won't interfere."

"I guess we better not say too much, Belle," said Mrs. Jeans. "Alvira asked us not to spread it."

Miss Jeans looked offended, and ceased to talk. Gamadge, wondering at what point discretion began in the Jeans opinion, rose.

"Well, then," he said, "I may tell my wife you'll do a

dress for her, and that there's a quilt in progress. And thank you so much."

Mrs. Jeans looked up at him. "You're welcome. I wouldn't want you to spread that refugee story, Mr. Gamadge; Alvira Radford didn't want it repeated."

"She only mentioned it to *us*," said Miss Jeans.

"And now she's dead. I'll remember."

If there were any suggestion of cause and effect here, neither Miss or Mrs. Jeans seemed to notice it. Gamadge took his leave, and when he rejoined his wife his face wore a smile.

"Did you find out anything?" she asked.

He turned the car, and drove up the Mill Road to Stratfield. "Yes. They'll make you a dress, and they're making you a patchwork quilt. It has pieces of the purple calico in it."

"You actually *saw*—"

"I did. There were two dresses and two sunbonnets. Gilbert Craye's private life was spied upon last summer by Miss Radford, and she confided in Mrs. and Miss Jeans. They have been stirred by the conviction that Craye is carrying on a love affair with a beautiful, married, blonde refugee—whom I had the pleasure of seeing this morning."

"But you said you thought he was in love with Fanny Hunter!"

"The Jeans ladies would inform you—at vast length and with few pauses for breath—that there is probably room for two love affairs in the life of such as Gilbert Craye; two or more, coincidental or successive. Mrs. and Miss Jeans do not like to think of the effect Craye's affair with a German refugee—if she is indeed a refugee—must have on China, Russia and England. They have gone so far as to appeal to the county authorities; Ledwell, I hope. I should like to see Mr. Ledwell consulted on such a delicate matter as that. We are not to spread the story, though."

"I shan't spread it!"

"You must be nice to your dressmaker and quilt maker; they have been useful. And you must invite Mrs. Groby to lunch."

"Oh," said Clara, faintly. "When?"

"Today, if we can catch her."

They went back to North Avebury by the reservation road, passed the cottage, and drove on to the Radford farm. Mrs. Groby came out to speak to them, again in working trim, and looking even more exhausted and wild than she had looked the day before. She said she would love to have lunch at the cottage.

"I hope Groby can come too," said Gamadge.

"He has an appointment in Stratfield, but he'll stop for me later. Wait a minute, he wants to speak to you. That dumb boy at the garage! Mr. Groby's all upset about what he said to you—it isn't so!"

Groby, who had been lurking in the hall, came out to elucidate. He seemed greatly embarrassed: "You sent me a message by that feller at my garage, Mr. Gamadge."

"Oh—did I?"

"I want to say that I was joking when I said what I did about what happened Saturday night at the cottage. I never meant it."

"Of course you didn't. I was annoyed at the moment, but I realized that you couldn't be expected to consider the feelings of total strangers. The Hunters might not have liked it, though."

"I want to apologize."

"Perfectly all right."

"Look here, Mr. Gamadge; my wife says you think of buying the cottage."

"When and if the mystery is cleared up, and if we can come to terms."

Groby said: "No trouble there. And as for the mystery, I've got a theory about that."

"Have you? That's good."

"I say that Aunt Alvira was hurt in that accident a good deal worse than old Knapp thought she was. He didn't make any kind of an examination of her that evening; he's a has-been, anyway. I've heard of cases when a man's neck was broken and he walked around for a week. That's what happened to Alvira; her neck was broken and she didn't know it; then she twisted it or something, and bingo!"

Mrs. Groby put her hands over her ears. Gamadge said: "Very ingenious notion; but Miss Radford's cervical vertebrae were broken in such a manner that the spinal column was injured; causing death. Thanks for the suggestion, though."

"I'm only trying to get that deed signed," said Groby, with an effort at his native jocularity.

"The sooner the better. Will you drive along with us now, Mrs. Groby?"

"Just let me get straightened out." She disappeared, and Groby, the picture of a hot, weary and dejected man, went down to the road and got into a new and glittering car. He drove glumly away.

Mrs. Groby soon reappeared, neat and even striking in her black dress and pumps and her fashionable little black hat and veil; she climbed into the Ford beside Clara, and made room for Gamadge. "I'm glad to be going somewheres," she said. "I just hate that place."

When they arrived at the cottage Gamadge shook up cocktails; Mrs. Groby seemed grateful for them.

"My, it's cute here," she said, looking around the living room. "I've never been inside since it was fixed."

"Those people in Hartford must be good," said Clara.

"Aunt Alvira must have spent a lot of money on it."

Mrs. Groby had a second Martini, and went in to lunch with her color high. Afterwards she followed Clara around the house, full of admiration for it. She was impressed, but perhaps a trifle disappointed, by the disappearance of the death room; agreed that Gamadge's inspiration certainly made the house more salable, or at worst rentable, and approved the opening of the back door. "I don't know," she said, "how you managed about garbage."

"I think Maggie lowered it out of a kitchen window."

"Crazy!"

The tour ended in Clara's bedroom, where Mrs. Groby sank down on the quilted counterpane with a sigh.

"It's cute, real cute; but I don't know how you can sleep with that waterfall going."

"We like it."

"And you don't mind lamps and candles and no electric icebox. Mis' Gamadge, you ought to have this cottage!"

"It almost seems so, doesn't it?"

"Mis' Gamadge—we got to sell it; we just got to."

"Have you, Mrs. Groby?" Clara looked at the distressed face of her guest, feeling uncomfortable.

"I just have to tell you. Aunt Eva Hickson's money's gone."

"Miss—Miss Radford's money?"

"The securities. They're not in the First National Bank in Stratfield, they're not anywhere. Don't tell."

"Are you sure?"

"There isn't even any box any more; I mean, they tell me Aunt Alvira gave it up back last October."

"She must have put the securities in some other bank."

"We can't find where. All those low-interest government bonds, good as money!" Tears began to form on Mrs. Groby's eyelashes; she got out a handkerchief. "It's bound to come out, I suppose, but don't mention it yet."

"Of course not. This is dreadful. You'll find them, Mrs. Groby, of course you will."

"Where? The bank had the list, has it yet; and Mr. Toms said she came and took the securities away with her in her black traveling bag, and gave up the key. All we have is her cash balance, and that isn't much, because she spent thousands fixing up this cottage and the farm."

"A hundred and six thousand dollars! It can't be gone!"

"It was only about seventy thousand after the taxes were all paid, but seventy thousand is a lot of money; and instead of seventy thousand all I have is this real estate and a few hundreds, and Mr. Groby went right out on Monday and paid cash for that new car; and of course he can't sell it back. We thought the seventy thousand was right in our pockets." .

"Mrs. Groby, I never heard anything so mean." Clara felt like crying too. "Won't you let me tell my husband? He does have such good ideas about such things."

"I want to tell him, because I want him to buy the cottage. I said that from the start," said Mrs. Groby, tears rolling down her face, "that Mr. Gamadge was a perfect jelman. He acted like a jelman right along, even after Mr. Groby talked so silly to our garage boy."

"Let's go down and tell him now."

They found Gamadge taking his ease on the porch. When he had heard the news he did not look surprised; he merely said: "It's a dam' shame. Sit down and have a cigarette, Mrs. Groby. Have you been looking for the securities at the farm?"

12

Schemes of Decoration

"We been tearing the place to pieces," said Mrs. Groby, her black-bordered handkerchief to her eyes. "Yesterday and to-day; we only found out yesterday; Mr. Toms at the bank felt quite bad when we asked about the box; he said he naturally thought Aunt Alvira had told me where the bonds were."

"Could she have been so foolish as to keep them in the house?"

"I wouldn't have said so, but I thought on account of the fence and the dogs she must have *some* money there."

"Of course the people who are looking after your affairs will make inquiries?"

"They don't know where to look. She hasn't deposited coupons or anything, she hasn't been near the Stratfield bank since she took the securities away. She had a few hundreds there still, but she hasn't drawn on her cash balance since she paid the last big bill for repairs, back last fall."

"And you've made a thorough search for cash at the farm?"

"Yes, but there isn't any locked-up place, or any place at all to keep valuables except a secret part of a closet, which I always knew about. You know those built-in cupboards, with doors above and doors below? There's one in Grandma Radford's bedroom, the one Aunt Alvira used after she moved back to the farm. Between the upper and bottom part there's a thick shelf, and it lifts up; there's a kind of a compartment under it, you'd never know. Grandma Radford kept her old jewelry and her silver spoons in it; she used to let me lift the lid up on rainy Sundays and look at the things. Of course I went right for that cupboard; all the old stuff is there, and some junk of Aunt Alvira's and Aunt Eva Hickson's; nothing else."

"You say Miss Radford took the securities out of the bank last fall?"

"October."

"That's quick work; it usually takes longer to settle an estate."

"The bank knew all about Aunt Eva Hickson's securities, and all about her business, and they knew there wouldn't be many outstanding debts, and there weren't any legacies except Aunt Alvira's. The cash balance would have taken care of bills, anyway. Aunt Alvira got possession in October, and took the securities out a week later—October fifteenth. Mr. Toms said he could have dropped; of course he thought she'd leave them right there. He bought most of 'em himself for Aunt Eva Hickson."

"And by that time the fence was up and the dogs on the rampage?"

"Yes, they came as soon as she moved back to the farm; in early September."

Gamadge pondered. "She didn't sink the seventy thousand in an annuity, I suppose?"

"We were afraid she had, but Mr. Toms said the income would be in checks, and where would she cash the checks? He's already called up the banks at Avebury and Stormer, and he's started on Hartford."

"Do you mean that she seems actually to have been paying her way in cash?"

"Ever since she drew checks for Yost, in Hartford, and the Avebury builders, and the plumbers. We don't know who fixed up the farm inside," said Mrs. Groby, looking curiously mystified, "but it must have cost money, more than was left in her balance. And we'll have to spend the rest of the balance," she added, her voice trembling, "for the funeral!"

"Tough on you, Mrs. Groby, very tough. One of the toughest things I ever heard of. Let's hope that the people at Stratfield will get on the track of those bonds."

"They're the kind that don't *leave* any track, Mr. Gamadge! They're just like money! But Mr. Toms is going to advertise—he has advertised; he started yesterday. Mr. Groby went over before lunch to inquire. We have to pay for that, too—the advertising, and the telephones, and everything. We *can't* hire a special man to do the tracing, because if we didn't get the bonds back, how could we pay him? You can imagine how I felt when you said you might buy the cottage."

"I can imagine. Miss Radford wasn't the type to go into wild financial schemes, was she? She wouldn't pay attention to fly-by-night brokers who called her up?"

"I wouldn't think so."

"Could she have made trips to Hartford or even to New York without its being known?"

"I should think Sam would know if she was ever away overnight. She could go to Hartford, I suppose; she used her car for long trips. She was just saving gas with that old rig she drove around in."

"Well, I must say I sympathize with you, Mrs. Groby."

"And on top of all that, they have the nerve to act as if I or Mr. Groby had killed Aunt Alvira for the seventy thousand!"

"Vexations of course; but when Miss Radford was killed you and Mr. Groby are supposed not to have known that the securities were missing. Or you might have known where Miss Radford had hidden them," added Gamadge. Mrs. Groby burst into a wail. Clara looked distressed, and Gamadge hastened to continue: "But we must look on the bright side of things, and hope that the murderer will be found when the bonds are. Meanwhile you have the farm and the cottage, and Groby has his garage business."

"But business is so awful now, and we couldn't even pay taxes on the real estate unless we got back our money."

"I've had a little experience in finding things, and I've seen how the police go about it; I wonder if you'd care to have me look the farm over? I might by some fluke locate Miss Radford's current cash for you."

"Oh, I wish you'd come right now!" Mrs. Groby started up, but Gamadge demurred:

"Let's wait and see what Groby thinks of it. He might object."

When Mr. Groby arrived, and was told that the Gamadges had heard about the seventy thousand dollars, he received the information with apathy; he seemed too hot and discouraged to care. Gamadge insisted on mixing him a gin collins. He sipped it thankfully (in his shirt sleeves by Clara's permission and against his wife's protest) and fanned himself with a newspaper.

"They can't find a trace of the bonds," he said. "I'm beginning to think old Alvira went crazy with so much money, and buried it. Some people have no confidence in banks, and now they're afraid of bombs, too. Gamadge, you can look for the stuff if you want to; very kind of you; but we didn't miss any tricks over there at the farm."

"I don't expect to find your securities," said Gamadge; "only what cash Miss Radford had in the house at the time she was killed. She must have been in the habit of keeping considerable amounts there, unless she was afraid of an attack by a personal enemy. There must have been some reason for that fence and those dogs."

Groby said: "They probably think Hattie and I have the money, and we're trying to beat taxes. Those fellows at Stratfield will say anything; they've got it in for me, and that's enough."

"I guess you wish now," said his wife in a nagging tone, "that you'd kept out of those side lines of yours. I begged you and begged you."

"But you didn't suggest moving into a smaller house and giving up the girl and some of your spending money," said Groby, in a tired voice. "Gamadge, if you'll take the cottage, ghost and all, you can have it and the property for five thousand cash."

"Just give me time, Groby."

"Time?" Groby looked at him, and then rose. "Might as well get going to the farm, anyhow."

The two couples drove to the farm in their two cars. Mrs. Groby unlocked the new oaken front door, and invited the Gamadges into a square entry from the back of which rose a steep flight of stairs. The stairs and the entry had been painted white, and neatly carpeted in gray. There was an old marble-topped side table against one wall, with an equally old mahogany-framed mirror above it.

"How nice," said Clara.

"Yes, but come in here—and don't faint!" Mrs. Groby, with a titter compounded of amusement and mortification, threw open the door on the left.

Gamadge did not faint, nor did Clara, but they were both astounded. The bay window which defaced the outside of the farm had been arched over within, and transformed what was once a dark farm parlor into a bright modern room. Below the window ran a half circle of upholstered bench, its upholstery a bright grass-green. The walls and ceiling were white, there was a large square mirror set into the plaster above the mantel, and on the mantelshelf was a bouquet of wax flowers under a glass. The smaller pieces of furniture were of glass and metal, the upholstered pieces were covered with a brilliant pattern of grass-green and pink; a carpet of even brighter pink concealed the ancient floor.

The wax bouquet was not the only relic of the past in this gay room; an immense round marble-topped table, artfully reduced in height, stood in the bay of the window; it upheld a large old lamp with a flowered china shade.

"We think," giggled Mrs. Groby, "that the decorator, whoever it was, must have been playing a joke on Aunt Alvira."

"Getting rid of stuff he couldn't sell to anybody else," muttered Groby.

"Well, but it's very clever," said Gamadge, staring about him. "Very charming."

"And how wonderful, to cut that great marble-topped thing down and make a coffee table of it," exclaimed Clara. "And what beautiful wax flowers; were they Miss Radford's?"

Mrs. Groby said that they had been in Grandma Radford's room. "Do you like the way this parlor is fixed up?" she asked, much surprised.

"In its way," said Gamadge, "I think it's delightful. You don't know who did it?"

"No, and we can't find the bill. I know one thing—Aunt Alvira never thought it up herself!"

"Did you ever ask her about it?"

"Yes, and she said it was the latest thing!"

"If the whole house had been done over like this it must have gouged a considerable chunk out of that seventy thousand."

"Only the dining room and the entry, thank goodness. There's a new bathroom upstairs, but the same plumbers did it that did the ones at the cottage."

"Let's see the dining room, by all means."

The dining room was across the entry; and if there was nothing playful about it, it was in its own way as amazing as the parlor. Its walls and ceiling were a pale, dull silver; it had a mulberry-colored rug, mauve curtains, and gray furniture. There were two purple-glass vases on the mantel, and there was a pink-lustre dish between them.

"It's a poem," said Gamadge. "I suppose those vases and that dish are family ornaments."

"Yes," replied Mrs. Groby, "and when I said the lavenders swore at each other, Aunt Alvira looked at me quite patronizing."

Gamadge said: "Somebody put her up to it all, of course; and what's more, somebody placed those wax flowers and those vases and that dish, and told her how to have the round table cut down, and made a feature of that gilt lamp with the china shade. Somebody that knew all about decoration—modern decoration. But that person must have had a lot of influence with her, and been very persuasive. That parlor does look like a joke, Mrs. Groby, but it looks to me like a shared joke; Miss Radford saw the fun of it too."

"I guess so, or she wouldn't have spent the money."

"But who was this somebody?"

The Grobys exchanged blank looks. Then Groby said: "Who did she know that knew about things like this?"

Mrs. Groby suddenly frowned. "Wait a minute. When I was on that war-knitting committee we met at Stratfield; we had our headquarters there. Somebody was talking about Gilbert Craye—they're always talking about Gilbert Craye in Stratfield, he fascinates them—and somebody else said he had the inside of his house restored; before his wife left him. I mean he had a man up from the Metropolitan Museum in New York to say what kind of curtains to have, and who to get to clean the pictures and mend the furniture."

"Fanny Hunter said something about his knowing a lot about decoration," said Clara, "and she ought to know, because she knows a lot about it herself."

Groby laughed in a disobliging manner. "Craye!" he said. "Gilbert Craye wouldn't know Alvira Radford was alive."

"Oh, is that so?" inquired Mrs. Groby. "That's all you know about it."

"Well, what do you know about it?" retorted her husband. "Buddies, were they—Craye and your Aunt Alvira?"

"He was right here in this house within a week after she moved in herself, last September!"

"Buying chickens."

"He has more chickens of his own than Aunt Alvira ever had. Aunt Alvira's girl told me about his being here. It was something about those refugees of his; the girl heard Aunt

Alvira say 'refugees,' and laugh; the girl thought he might have been trying to board some of 'em out on Aunt Alvira."

"And do her decorating for her if she'd take a couple off his hands?" Groby seemed amused.

"I'm just telling you. I mentioned him and the refugees to Aunt Alvira, but she turned it off; she never liked anybody asking her questions."

"I think that's all nonsense," said the frank Groby. "Know what I think? Some smart salesman came up and talked the old lady into the whole business. The stores read about wills in the papers, and find out who get legacies, and they're right after the heirs, especially women alone in the world. It's a regular racket."

"Like when the man called you up on Monday about that new car," said Mrs. Groby.

"That was no racket; that car was the biggest bargain I ever saw, and I've traded cars most of my life."

Gamadge said: "Might Sam know anything about new furniture coming in?"

Sam was found by Groby in the cow yard, and brought in. He looked gloomily about the mulberry dining room, and said that long-distance vans had come up in the middle of the preceding October. He was not required to help, indeed almost never set foot within the house, and knew nothing about the decorating. "Only the vans had a big K on 'em."

He was allowed to leave the room before Gamadge and Clara said in chorus: "Keene!"

"Keene?" demanded Mrs. Groby.

"Keene in New York," Gamadge told her. "Furniture and decorating."

"And if this room and the parlor were in their model house," said Clara, "all Miss Radford would have to do would be to order them duplicated, rugs and curtains and all."

"Keene has a model house in the store," Gamadge explained to Mrs. Groby. "It's done over every year. But Miss Radford never ordered the rooms from Keene's illustrated catalogue; never. Not on her own. Well, let's tackle the lost securities problem. Had Miss Radford any kind of office with a desk?"

"They're not in her desk," Mrs. Groby led the party

back to the gay parlor, and through it into a small room which had not lost its original walnut, patent rocker, and threadbare carpet. A tall and ugly walnut desk stood open, its contents strewn on an adjoining table.

"Not a thing here but old bills and checkbooks, and some junk," said Groby. "And there isn't any secret drawer, either. I'm mechanic enough to know that."

"Mind if I look these over?"

"Go to it."

There was not much; Miss Radford had not treasured old papers, and hers seemed to have been a limited and an arid life. The last voucher in the half-filled checkbook was dated November, 1941.

"She actually seems to have paid cash for everything since November thirtieth of last year," said Gamadge.

"There isn't a bill here for 1942," Groby informed him.

"Remarkable. Here are the big bills for the builders and painters and plumbers, and for Yost's work at the cottage. Here's a smaller bill for an extra painting job, and one for building in that bench under the bay window—both dated October."

"That bunch of letters isn't interesting," said Mrs. Groby. "They're all real old, except one or two. There's one from Aunt Eva Hickson, about coming to live in the cottage after her husband died."

Gamadge found and read it, a dour communication, seven years old. It said that the sisters might as well set up housekeeping together and save expenses; that the writer expected Alvira to run the house—she herself was arthritic and used to service, and wouldn't be able to turn a hand. In return, Mrs. Hickson proposed to lift the mortgage on the farm, pay taxes and upkeep on both properties, and foot all bills. The letter ended: "You're getting the best of the bargain, but I need care, and I don't like strangers."

Gamadge replaced it in its envelope, which was postmarked Cincinnati. He said: "Your aunt Alvira seems to have earned her legacy."

"I guess she did; still, Aunt Eva Hickson wasn't as dry as she writes."

"Were they on affectionate terms, so far as you know?"

"You can't tell what terms folks like that are on. They never fought; at least I never heard that they did."

"Old stick, Eva Hickson," said Groby. "I never could stand her."

The desk had held few oddments; a dog whistle, rubber bands which broke when stretched, bits of old red sealing wax, pens, old Christmas cards carefully preserved, church circulars. Old leases for the farm and the new one for the cottage were in a long envelope. There was no address book or list of telephone numbers.

An arid life, Gamadge thought; had Miss Radford lately hoped to brighten it?

"Let's go upstairs," he said. "I think Miss Radford would keep valuables upstairs, where she could snatch them in case of fire."

"That's what we thought." Mrs. Groby led the way up to the second floor, and into a long northwest bedroom which looked as though it had been hit by a bomb.

13

Try the Impossible

Mr. and Mrs. Groby had made a job of it. The bedding had been torn from the bed and the mattress rolled up, drawers had been removed from dressers and turned upside down, rag rugs were piled in corners, clothing was heaped upon chairs, all the closet doors stood open, soot that had fallen down the chimney drifted across the hearth.

"There ain't any loose floor boards," said Mrs. Groby, "or any holes in the chimney, or any ripped-up places in the pillows or the mattress."

Groby, lifting a picture to its hook, said that if there was money in the room, Alvira had certainly buried it good and deep.

"She wouldn't bury it deep." Gamadge stood with his hands in his pockets, looking about him. "She wouldn't nail it up anywhere. She was using it for current expenses, and—as I said—she'd want to get at it in a hurry in case of fire." He went across the room to a built-in cupboard; its upper and lower doors hung wide. "This where your grandmother had her cache?"

"Yes." The others joined him, and Mrs. Groby lifted a lid in the partition shelf between the top and bottom halves. "See how tight this fits. You'd never know there was a join."

"But the secret seems to have been an open one in the family. Your grandmother wouldn't expect a child to keep it." Gamadge peered into a shallow rectangular space which contained old leather and velvet boxes, a lacquered tray full of bright Californian shells, daguerreotypes, some thin old silver spoons tied together in a bundle, and a large silver watch.

"No, everybody knew about it," said Mrs. Groby, "but outsiders didn't."

Gamadge opened the boxes. One contained a pair of gold filigree earrings, one a gold bracelet, one a cameo brooch. The last one was filled to overflowing with a silver head-necklace, a silver-gilt stick pin and a couple of rings; the rings had small stones in them; one a diamond cluster, one a row of sapphires and rubies.

"That box was Aunt Eva Hickson's," said Mrs. Groby.

Gamadge said: "Did your grandmother keep money here?"

"I never saw any."

"Guess she didn't handle much," said Groby. "She might not have seen a dollar bill from one year to another."

"She did too, Walt! I often heard her talk about her egg money she saved."

"Then she put it in the savings bank."

Gamadge said: "Well, I don't know." He stood looking down at the neatly fashioned cavity, a smile on his lips. "Do you believe, Mrs. Groby, that lightning never strikes twice in the same place?"

"Do I what?"

"Let's see whether Grandma Radford told you all her secrets." He got a knife out of his pocket, opened the larger blade, and inserted the point into a faintly visible crack in the old paint-work. The whole bottom of the cavity rose; it was a thin board, and it had covered a second cavity a scant inch deep. The jewel boxes slid to one end of their upper hiding place, and there was a rattle of small shells.

"False bottom!" Groby spoke hoarsely, pushing his flushed face forward.

"As neat a trick as ever I saw, and I shouldn't have seen it if the wood hadn't warped a little. A cache within a cache," said Gamadge, scooping up a layer of paper money and crushing it into Mrs. Groby's trembling hands.

Groby snatched at falling greenbacks, and began wildly to count them. At last he and Mrs. Groby had the whole treasure assembled in a sheaf, and Mrs. Groby looked up at Gamadge, her face crimson: "Nine hundred and ninety-five dollars!"

"Did Miss Radford have a handbag with her when she was taken into the cottage?" he asked.

"Yes, old Duckett has it," panted Groby. "Three dollars and some change in it."

"Then we'll say that Miss Radford was in possession of a thousand in cash by the first of July."

"Well, Mr. Gamadge, all I can say is that we're obliged to you. Can't say how long it would have been before we found it ourselves." Groby could not take his eyes from the sheaf in his wife's fingers; he patted his forehead with his handkerchief.

"We never would have found it!" Mrs. Groby raised her face from adoring contemplation of her money to scowl at him. "Never!"

"I always like to have one try at the impossible." Gamadge was looking pleased with himself.

Mrs. Groby gazed at him, gazed down at her money, and then addressed him in a voice of sudden anguish: "Mr. Gamadge—ought I take it now?"

"What do you mean, take it now?" Groby stared at her as if personally affronted. "It's yours, isn't it?"

She paid no attention to him, but continued to search Gamadge's sympathetic features. "I mean, ought I to hand it over to Mr. Toms or somebody till he gets the tax man?"

"Well: that would be the correct procedure, of course," said Gamadge. "It's part of Miss Radford's estate, and the will isn't even probated yet."

Groby, much alarmed, protested violently: "What is this—a charity board? We've just lost the whole estate, this is all we're going to get. And boy, we need it! And I tell you what, Gamadge, you're entitled to a commission; ten percent. Right now, if you like."

Gamadge, ignoring this, continued to address Mrs. Groby: "I'm merely answering your question as to the correct legal procedure; and that procedure would certainly make an excellent impression on all concerned. But it's none of our business, Clara's and mine; we won't mention this."

Groby stood perspiring. "We lost seventy thousand," he said, and his voice faltered.

Mrs. Groby burst out crying. "I've had enough of monkey business, Walter Groby; if it wasn't for all the monkey business we wouldn't be in so bad now. You want to do something Mr. Gamadge wouldn't do?"

Gamadge said: "The Gamadges haven't had as much bad luck as you have—financially; we can adopt a high moral tone and convince ourselves that we could maintain a high moral attitude against adversity. But I recommend turning in the money. Have you enough to go on with until you get probate?"

"Sure we have," said Groby. "We're not bankrupt."

"Then we'd better drive right over to Stratfield now," said his wife.

Groby mumbled, "Banks closed."

"Well, we know where Mr. Toms lives, don't we?"

Gamadge said: "And we must be going. We promised Maggie that we wouldn't leave her in the cottage alone after sunset."

He and Clara took their leave, the Grobys staring rather confusedly at them. When they were on the way home, Clara said: "Poor Mr. Groby."

"Now don't you get sentimental about Groby; he tried to bribe me with ninety-nine dollars and fifty cents."

"He can't help being that way. I wish you could find the rest of the seventy thousand."

"Think how awful Groby would be with seventy thousand dollars."

"He might be nicer."

Gamadge looked at her, smiled, and took a hand off the wheel to pat the top of her head.

As they reached the cottage the telephone was ringing. It had stopped by the time they arrived on the porch, and Maggie came out to say that Mr. Hunter was on the wire.

"Glad I caught you," he told Gamadge. "We want you and Clara to perform a rescue job this evening; we are threatened with dinner guests—Craye and one of his refugees."

"I hope it's the wandering princess from a Gothic tale?"

Hunter laughed. "Yes—Mrs. Star; that describes her. I may have found her a job, and they're coming to talk it over. But I found her two other jobs, and neither seemed to suit."

"I didn't realize until I called on him this morning that he was harboring refugees."

"He's very reticent about them; we don't mention them unless he does."

"Why should he be reticent?"

"I believe it's because they all have hostages or something. Don't ask me about them—ask him."

"I don't think I should be rewarded for my indiscretion. Wait a minute while I speak to Clara."

He returned to the telephone to say that Clara and he would be delighted to dine. "But," he added, "will Craye and Mrs. Star be delighted?"

"Yes. He said you'd met her this morning."

"Met her? She opened the door for me, and nearly froze me on the mat." Gamadge added: "Perhaps because she's the niece of a cardinal?"

"Her race isn't as adaptable as some others. Well, thanks for coming. Shall we send down for you?"

"Certainly not; most kind and obliging of you to suggest it, but you need your own gas. We're bringing Maggie."

Gamadge hung up, and went to ask Maggie if she had had time to do anything about his other shirt. She had two pieces of good news for him; his large bag had come by railway express, and there was a telegram from the Herons. It said: STANDING BY SHALL ARRIVE AS PLANNED UNLESS NOTIFIED TO THE CONTRARY LOVE TO BOTH FROM DICK AND SALLY

"Aren't they sports?" Clara was pleased.

"Yes. I suppose that now I have the clothes I must dress for the Hunters."

"They dress all the time."

"First we'll have our splash in the pool."

But he waited to put in a long telephone call to Duckett. Ten minutes later he and Clara were in the pool, and an hour later they had arrived at Mountain Ridge Farm.

It was like walking out of a rustic vignette into an

academy oil of *Life at the Manor* to pass in ten minutes
from the homely dusk of the cottage into the Hunters'
yellow drawing room. The party was already drinking
cocktails, and a striking party it was. Phineas Hunter,
always elegant, was—oddly enough—not so elegant in
evening clothes as Gilbert Craye. Craye, finished as a
drawing in sepia, black, and white, his face thin as a coin,
his manner so much part of himself as to seem no manner
at all, had regained his mood of perpetual laughter; he
seemed much pleased that the Gamadges were there.

And if he drew the eye away from Hunter, Mrs. Star's
silvery fairness put Fanny Hunter's blonde fairness into
the shade. Mrs. Star's features, untouched by rouge or
powder, were sharp and delicate as if cut by the finest
tools from white shell or agate. The pale gray of her eyes
was repeated in her thin cotton dress, which flowed from
her sloping shoulders as though it had been made of China
crêpe. Against Fanny's brilliant colors she was an engraving.

She seemed to be engaged in extracting from Fanny the
details of Miss Radford's accident and death. When she
and Clara were introduced, she looked concerned and
sympathetic.

"I do hope the haunting is over," she said. "It must have
been the worst kind; we have them in Europe a great
deal."

"We don't have them here at all," said Fanny earnestly.

"You do not?" Mrs. Star looked surprised. "I thought
you did. I thought the Indians had them, and that spiritual-
ism was invented in America."

Hunter murmured in Gamadge's ear: "It is not a race
famous for tact."

"We had some friends in Poland," continued Mrs. Star,
in her soft, barely accented voice, "whose castle was
dreadfully haunted."

"Did they move away?" asked Fanny, in a quavering
voice.

"Oh, they could not; it was their hereditary home. Of
course it's gone now, quite gone, and so is the family; but
the manifestations had been going on for centuries. On a
certain day of the year the children were sent to Warsaw,
because the ghost was known to be dangerous at that time.
Mrs. Gamadge," she turned silvery-gray eyes on Clara,
"what is a sunbonnet?"

Hunter murmured: "Shall we rescue your wife?" but Clara was describing a sunbonnet with calm detachment.

At dinner, Hunter was immensely amused at Clara's description of the improvements at the Radford farm. Fanny said: "Of course Mrs. Groby is right; of course you helped her, Gil! Why didn't you tell us?"

Craye took this humor in good part. He said: "I would have if she'd asked me. I'm an expert since those fellows came up and lectured me on my house. The house certainly needed help; you ought to have seen it, Mrs. Gamadge, when it had all the plush and the marbles in the parlor. And there was a Crusader on the newel post. I didn't want things done wrong, so I read up a little. We found stuff in the attics and barns, and they restored the mouldings and the paneling. I got samples for curtain materials—quite fun it was," he ended, on a note of languor.

Fanny Hunter said in Gamadge's ear: "His awful wife—nobody could put up with her, and she had to be amused. But as soon as the work was finished, off she went. Gil had to bring suit to keep the baby, and then it died, and she made a frightful row. She was going to write a book—I mean somebody was going to write it for her, but Gilbert bought her off."

"Has Craye found his refugee a job this time?"

"Well, I'm afraid not; it's so difficult. She isn't trained for anything, Henry; she could only be a companion; and I don't *see* her as a companion, do you?"

"Not clearly, no."

"People want somebody to read to them, and play games with, and do all kinds of errands. And they want to talk about the war with their friends; and how could they? Mrs. Star's husband is *fighting*. No matter how much of a brute he is, or how much she loathes him, people couldn't say all they felt, could they?"

"Not quite all, perhaps."

"Her own people had a dreadful time, and Baron von Stermi wouldn't lift a finger for them. Oh dear, now I've given it away, and I promised Gil I wouldn't!"

"I shall keep the lady's real name even from Clara."

"Oh, please do."

"Von You-Know-Who is of the old officer caste; I don't think it would have helped if he had lifted a finger."

"Oh, isn't it all a mix-up? And now Phineas got old Mr.

Tremblow to say he'd try her as a secretary, but she can't type!"

"Very discouraging."

"There's one thing, I don't think Gil cares whether she gets a job or not; he's wonderful about his refugees."

"Does she care whether she gets a job or not?"

"I don't know."

But it soon became apparent that if Mrs. Star had not been trained in a business school, she had been trained rigorously in another. When coffee had been drunk she was asked to play and sing; she did so promptly, and almost professionally; in fact, her performance was so dazzling that Fanny refused to follow her at the piano.

"Too bad there's no living to be made that way," sighed Hunter. "Let's have some bridge."

For the first rubber Mrs. Star cut in with the three men. She explained without embarrassment that she could not play for stakes.

"Not much of a gamble to carry you, Mrs. Star," said Craye. And it soon became evident that here again she had graduated from a tough school; she played with firmness but audacity, and she and Craye made the most of their cards and came out well ahead. Gamadge arranged a return party for the following night.

"I shall like to see the cottage," said Mrs. Star.

"There'll be no ghost, you know."

"I hope not."

When the Gamadges were driving home, Maggie again in the rumble, Clara said: "I hope you didn't think I was wrong to talk about those decorations at the Radford farm, Henry."

"Not at all. I only wish you'd gone on to ask Craye what he called on Miss Radford for last September."

"I wouldn't have for anything!"

"How do you like Mrs. Star?"

"Is it because she's been through so much that she seems—so different from other people?"

"How different?"

"She doesn't seem quite human to me. I don't mean that she's *in*human, either."

"Unhuman, rather."

"Yes—a little."

"An undine; no soul?" Gamadge smiled at her.

"Not that, either. I can't explain."

"A strong, controlled spirit."

"She simply couldn't be a companion to some nice old rich lady."

Gamadge laughed outright. "Perhaps she's strong enough and controlled enough even for that."

As they were going up to bed the telephone rang. Gamadge answered it: "Hello, Mrs. Groby!"

"I just wanted to tell you, Mr. Gamadge; I went—Mr. Duckett took me to the burying ground tonight. I'm just back home."

"Oh—how trying for you, though."

"I thought I ought to, Mr. Gamadge; I'm the only member of the family left, and I thought I ought to be there." She swallowed audibly. "I don't know why I felt so bad; I didn't care for either of them much, or they for me, but it was terrible. Like a funeral going backwards."

"You did the right thing; of course you're upset."

"There wasn't a soul to see it, except the men with that van they have; and Mr. Duckett told me to tell you they wouldn't have to have it done at Hartford, there was going to be somebody at Stratfield hospital tomorrow morning; or is it this morning?"

"Yes, it's after twelve. You must be worn out after the day you've had."

"I thought I'd feel better if I talked to you. I hope I didn't wake you up?"

"No indeed; I'm a night bird. Very good of you to call me."

"I wanted to tell you that Mr. Duckett says they all appreciate it very much—my turning that money in. Mr. Gamadge, I didn't half thank you for finding it."

"Glad I did."

"Mr. Duckett thinks it means Aunt Alvira hadn't been robbed of those securities, and killed to prevent her finding out; because she would have kept them where she kept the money, if they were in the house at all."

"So she would."

"Mr. Gamadge—*where are they?*"

"Perhaps we'll find out."

14

An Exorcism

At two o'clock on the morning of Friday the tenth the weather broke with a tremendous crash; Gamadge, waked by it, lurched about closing the bedroom door and windows that faced the west. He had already heard the drum and rush of the rain, now he saw it by lightning—a steely curtain blown past the cottage in waves.

He went into the farther bedroom, listened until he was sure Maggie's footsteps were pounding about overhead, and closed those windows too. No earthly waterfall could be heard above this cataract. When he returned to the north room he went to the east doorway; rivulets were already beginning to trickle down the hillside.

In the morning it was still pouring. Maggie was distressed. She had important errands to be done in Avebury, too important to be entrusted to any delivery boy; if a cardinal's niece were expected to dinner, for instance, there must be a mighty fish course. Gamadge said he would drive in; he had meant to do so in any case—he had telephoning to do that was not for Clara's ears.

He shut himself into a booth in a drugstore and called his friend Robert Macloud at that gentleman's summer fastness in Vermont. Macloud said no, he read no papers while he was on vacation. He got his news on the radio—as much as he could stand of it. "What's in the papers that I ought to have seen? Something about you? You seem to have got back safely, anyhow; congratulations."

"I got back safely. Could you possibly come over to Connecticut this Sunday? Place north of Avebury."

"You'll have to do better than that; what's Avebury?"

"Place north of Hartford. I think there'll be an inquest on Monday, and I'd like you to be present."

"Inquest? On who?"

"Nobody you know; but Clara's a witness."

"What does she want a lawyer there for?"

"It was a homicide. I wasn't here, and she has a queer story. Somebody ought to be on hand to see that she isn't unnecessarily heckled. Ledwell—the Stratfield state's attorney—is a young fellow, very keen on his job; I think he's going to follow up with an arrest and a trial, if he can."

"Arrest *Clara?*"

"If there's a trial, she'll get a verdict of guilty but insane."

"Great heavens, Gamadge, what are you telling me?"

"It may not come to that, but I have to be ready for it. I don't want her confused at the inquest. I don't want people thinking there's something wrong with her."

"Great heavens, no wonder you sound as though you'd been chewing alum!"

"I've been eating ashes for about four days, and keeping up a front."

"Nice homecoming for you."

"That doesn't matter. Can you get here by Sunday?"

"I'd come today, only I have a man with me. I'll get rid of him, if you like, and drive down now."

"No, Sunday will do. I hate to break into your vacation."

"Don't talk nonsense."

"We can discuss the thing on Sunday. I needn't tell you that I'm doing what I can at this end, but I doubt if I can manage anything effective in the time; however, I dug up something yesterday that gave me a possible lead. Who's that fellow you told me was such a whiz at tracing financial deals and illegal sales of bonds, and so on?"

"Lovsky."

"Could you get hold of him and start him working for me on Monday?"

"I'll call the office."

"No hope of getting him this week, I suppose?"

"Not unless by some miracle he's in his New York quarters. He's all over the place, you know. I only hope he isn't smothered in some war job."

"Well, get hold of somebody, if you can; it shouldn't be too difficult a job, but the trouble is that it may take some time. Tricky; it means finding the real financial rating of somebody, and a lot of undercover work. I want Lovsky particularly because you said he knew how to work on the quiet."

"He does. He's the original bolt from the blue. Er—he comes high, you know."

"Do you think that matters while I have a dollar, or a dollar's worth of credit?"

"Naturally not; I'm just telling you." Macloud paused. "Sure you'll have to do all the financing?"

"You mean can I push it off on the state of Connecticut? Not unless I have a stroke of luck. I wish I could go more into detail, but I've said more than I ought, now."

"Take it easy. I'll see you on Sunday before lunch."

Gamadge told him how to find the cottage, and rang off. He returned home with a magnificent piece of salmon and the makings of hors d'oeuvres, besides a bundle of rain-washed rosebuds. Flowers had been a problem, but the woman at the nursery had waded out in rubber boots and a mackintosh and cut the roses for him.

After lunch the rain ceased; the waterfall could be heard roaring. By three o'clock Gamadge made Clara put on a bathing suit and walk around the property with him; he said that if he had to buy it he might as well know what he was getting for his money. The tour ended, he sat on the dividing wall at the bottom of the slope behind the house, and looked up at the ridge and its flanking woods.

"I never saw better ground for an advance or a retreat," he said. "The woman in the sunbonnet could leave a car along the reservation road or above or below the farms on the highway. She could cut through the woods across the stream, or through those woods up there and behind the ridge, or circle the north end of the cottage. She wouldn't be seen, and the trips wouldn't take more than a few minutes either way. That purple dress is a kind of smock thing; buttons down the front. You could get out of it in a second."

Clara said that it was almost worse to think that a human being had been doing it than to think it was a ghost.

A fine sunset and a rosy sky welcomed the dinner guests when they drove up for early cocktails. The cottage was festive; a little iron table was set out on the porch with canapés, and Gamadge stood in the yard with the shaker in his hand, its glass and chromium twinkling in the rays of the evening light. The guests stood about on the grass to eat and drink. They looked exotic in that setting, beings from another world.

"It is perfect; it is charming," said Mrs. Star to Gamadge. "You know how to live. It looks so simple, and really it means so much complicated preparation. I hear a waterfall."

"Yes, it's booming today. Like to see it?"

"I should love to."

"If you won't spoil your dress—there's long grass."

Mrs. Star, lifting her pale-gray skirt a little disdainfully, said that if it were spoiled she could soon make another. They crossed the road and went along a rough track that led them under trees and out upon a flat stone. She stood looking at the surging water, and the dark pool below.

"This is what I like."

"You are the genius loci."

"Am I?"

"But I hope your wicked uncle won't make the waterfall drown the lot of us."

"I have no malign spirits in my family; and in any case, Undine turned it all back into a stream again. The setting is wrong, Mr. Gamadge, for your fancy; this is no tributary of the Danube."

"I dare say the whole look of it is different."

"The feel of it is different."

She stood poised in her floating dress, an image out of the dead past; literally and forever, she had no background of her own. Of course she was different.

They went back to the cottage. Dinner was lively, there was much approving talk about the transformation of the little bedroom—"I was simply dreading it," said Fanny Hunter, "and now it isn't even there!"—and everybody agreed that the Gamadges had been right to stick to the cottage.

When they were at coffee in the living room a faint swish of tires on grass and a bump against the porch preceded Maggie's entrance with an announcement: "It's a boy on a bicycle. He has an envelope for Mr. Gamadge, and he won't give it to me. He says he's to put it into Mr. Gamadge's hands himself."

Gamadge went out. When he came back he had a smile on his face and a long envelope in his hands. As he advanced, he took several sheets of typing from the envelope, and glanced at them.

"Splendid," he said. "Shall we put off bridge for half an hour, and have an exorcism?"

Everybody looked surprised, but only Mrs. Star spoke. She asked after a moment, gravely, "You are joking?"

"Not at all. With these papers in my hand I can exorcise the ghost of Mrs. Hickson out of this cottage."

"Please don't joke about an exorcism, Mr. Gamadge."

"I'm speaking in symbols, Mrs. Star." Gamadge sat down beside a lamp, and spread his papers out on the table. "The sheriff of Avebury is a great fellow, and he's done a great job. I thought you might all like to hear about it."

"I shall," said Hunter. He sat beside his wife on the sofa; Craye was on Fanny's left, Mrs. Star between him and Clara. Maggie came in and put up a side table; then she went out and brought in a tray with whiskey, a siphon, and tumblers.

Craye, watching her, said: "We all will. The fewer ghosts the better; we don't need 'em. There are too many people in the world, let's eliminate ghosts."

Hunter, raising an eyebrow, said: "As a pillar of the First Congregational Church of Avebury, let me protest against these Malthusian heresies. You Stratfield heathen are getting far too cynical, Craye."

Mrs. Star said: "Mr. Craye has every reason to think that there are too many people."

Craye flushed a little, his eyes still on the whiskey. "I withdraw the remark," he said, "but I say remove the ghosts."

"I'll remove one," said Gamadge, "here and now. This letter from Duckett informs me that the autopsy on Mrs. Hickson was performed this morning."

"On Mrs. Hickson?" Craye stared.

"Yes. She was exhumed privately last night, and a toxicologist performed a belated autopsy today. Her body contains no arsenic."

Hunter said: "You let no grass grow under your feet. I congratulate you."

"Further examinations will be carried on," continued Gamadge, "but there seems to be no question in the case of any poison but arsenic; Mrs. Hickson's symptoms rule other poisons out. No arsenic, no murder; Mrs. Hickson died a natural death, and her ghost had no cause to avenge itself upon Alvira Radford. Therefore, no ghost."

Fanny said eagerly: "We said there was nothing in that poisoning story; didn't we, Clara?"

Clara nodded, her eyes on Gamadge.

"But what must have been Alvira Radford's feelings last Saturday evening," he went on, smiling at her, "when she saw a figure, clothed in her sister's old purple dress and sunbonnet, surge up at the corner of the cottage; at the moment, you will remember, when the Radford buggy was full of flowers for that sister's grave? Of course she fainted, and of course, when she regained consciousness, she didn't want to enter this haunted place. But afterwards she pulled herself together; if there was a ghost, it could not harm her.

"Clara will tell you that Miss Radford had already shown dislike for the cottage, and had refused to enter it. I have good reason to suppose, from certain evidence, that she had the unhappiest memories of her life here—years of slavery under the domination of a cold, penurious, selfish woman. When she moved back to her old home she left her sister's personal possessions behind; she even left the furniture that they had used here and the pictures they had looked at. Her instincts were against burning up wearable clothing or even giving it away; but she had put off dealing with it."

"But the apparition still might have been a ghost," said Mrs. Star, "even if it didn't kill Miss Radford. It might have come to warn her."

"You may feel strongly persuaded that that is true," said Gamadge, "when I tell you that the garments in the attic, to which a flesh-and-blood murderer might have had access, cannot have been worn by any person since they were worn by Eva Hickson; their knots and creases prove it."

Mrs. Star inhaled a long breath, and Fanny Hunter shrank against her husband. He patted her shoulder.

"Trust Gamadge, my dear," he said. "He has promised to remove the ghost for us."

"I could only suppose, when I saw those knots and creases," said Gamadge, "that there must be another set of purple garments; purple, sprigged with black. There is. Two sets, exactly alike, were made for Mrs. Hickson by dressmakers named Jeans, who lived in Stratfield, or near it, and whose address was kindly supplied to me yesterday by Mr. Gilbert Craye."

Craye, with a smile like a faint grimace, murmured: "What a fellow you are."

"Not at all; the clothes had been finished by hand, the Jeans women were dressmakers and friends of Miss Radford, Miss Radford seems to have possessed no sewing machine. Logic forced me to call upon Mrs. and Miss Jeans. I saw pieces of the material in a quilt, and Duckett says here that he now has a scrap in his possession, found in the Jeans piece bag. Yesterday I was not ready to be quite frank with the Jeans family; I had no other line of inquiry to pursue, and I could only hope that if I kept my search for the other dress and sunbonnet a secret the murderer might not destroy it, and it might be found. But that was a forlorn hope at best; the territory to be searched is too vast, the murderer too cunning. All I have done was to lay the ghost. Or have I laid it?" He looked at Mrs. Star.

She slowly bent her head. "Yes. I relinquish the ghost now. Someone else wore those things, and it was a frightful plot."

"But are you stuck now, Henry," asked Mrs. Hunter with childlike anxiety, "and can't you do anything more?"

"Well, I was stuck yesterday morning," confessed Gamadge, "but in the afternoon that line of inquiry that I was hoping for presented itself. I won't bore you with it."

"Bore us?" Hunter, laughing heartily, waved his hand. "Look at your audience!"

"Do you really want me to go on with this?" Gamadge's eyes passed from him to Fanny, on to Mrs. Hunter, and then to Craye. There was a chorus.

"Well, then; but first we must refresh ourselves."

He went into the kitchen, and came back with ice. When drinks had been mixed and distributed, he sat down with his own glass at his elbow and a cigarette between his fingers. He got a notebook out of his pocket, consulted it, and laid it down.

"What I needed," he said, "was some faint indication of a motive for this most curious crime. And what I asked myself first of all was whether the murderer's object had or had not been achieved. I inferred that it had; in fact, I looked upon the case as an end-game in chess: problem, to mate in three moves. The first move, Miss Radford's accident and its result—her immobilization in the little green bedroom with the latchless door. By this move a pawn was sacrificed—Clara.

"Move two, Miss Radford's murder; a piece was taken, the Queen.

"Move three—what was move three?"

"But wasn't Miss Radford's death the end of the game, then?" asked Fanny.

"No; Miss Radford had to die, but her death didn't end the game, Fanny. Why that most remarkable masquerade, why all those circumstances of confusion and terror, if Miss Radford's death were the end of the game? I was confused myself, I can tell you, until I learned yesterday afternoon from Mrs. Groby that Miss Radford's securities, inherited last summer from Mrs. Hickson and amounting—taxes paid—to about seventy thousand dollars, had completely disappeared."

15

Line of Inquiry

"Oh, good heavens," protested Hunter, "the unfortunate Grobys!"

"Unless they took them, Phin." Mrs. Hunter, very alert, sat up straight to interrogate Gamadge: "Where are they missing *from*, Henry?"

"Well, that's the trouble; we don't know. We only know that Miss Radford herself took them out of her safe deposit box last October—as soon, in fact, as she got her hands on the estate."

"But where was the box?"

Gamadge turned a smiling look on Craye. "In Stratfield."

Craye had already come to the end of his highball. It seemed to have done him good; he also sat up straighter, got out his glasses, put them on, and returned his host's look with a firm, judicial one. "The securities are not missing," he said in a corrective tone. "They have been exchanged. The money's been reinvested."

"If it has," said Gamadge, "Miss Radford has left no trace of the transaction anywhere. The natural place for such memoranda would be her desk at the farm; but nothing of the kind is there, although it contains her other business papers."

"You don't get cash out of the air, you know," Craye informed him with polite condescension. "You deposit the coupons, or you cash the dividend checks."

"But Miss Radford hasn't been depositing coupons or cashing dividend checks—or any other checks—in Avebury, in Stormer or in Stratfield. Or," said Gamadge, referring to the second of the typed papers on the table beside him, "so far as Toms of Stratfield has been able to discover, in Hartford."

"Then what on earth has she been paying her expenses with?"

"With cash. Odd, isn't it? Have another highball."

Craye allowed his glass to be refilled. His attitude relaxed, and one long hand lay passive on the arm of his chair as the other conveyed the tumbler to his mouth. Mrs. Star's eyes were on him. She said: "Perhaps she converted the securities into currency, and was hoarding it."

"Well, no, I don't think so." Gamadge, having attended to the wants of his other guests, resumed his seat. "She kept money on hand, but I found it. It amounted to nearly a thousand dollars, and I imagine that that's all she had on the premises at the time of her death. She was undoubtedly receiving cash from some source unknown."

Mrs. Star slowly turned her eyes away from Craye and upon Gamadge. "How very extraordinary."

"Is it not? Since the thirtieth of last November she has not filled out a check, or paid a bill with one."

Craye said: "You're going to try to trace those bonds."

"Well, the trouble is they were all bearer bonds; I am not sure that they will ever be traced."

"Then," declared Fanny Hunter with bright finality, "You're stuck again!"

Hunter imprisoned her hand in his. "My child, does Gamadge look to you as if he were stuck?"

"If I am," said Gamadge, "it's not in that quicksand. I'm going at the mystery from a different angle."

Mrs. Star, since she had abandoned the supernatural in favor of the mundane, had become practical and cool, as if concentrating on an abstract problem of some interest. She said: "You will try to find out who is paying her income."

"Was, Mrs. Star. She is dead, and the income need be paid no longer."

"Of course. You make it all so vivid, for the moment she lived again."

"And of course," said Gamadge, "I could not but relate the two oddities in her behavior of last autumn; she withdrew her securities, and at about the same time she carried out those remarkable changes at the farm. I did not think it unreasonable to conclude that there was one influence at work in both cases. Duckett has been invaluable." He picked up one of the typed sheets and ran his eye over it. "He has tackled the painters, plumbers and builders, Yost in Hartford, and Keene in New York; and he gives me the following facts:

"Yost's job was over when they finished the cottage; the plumbers' job was over when they finished the bathrooms at the cottage and at the farm. But shortly after the painters and builders had left the farm—early in September it was—she called up to request further work from them. She wanted the bay window in the living room arched over, and a bench built under it; and she wanted silver paint on the dining-room walls and ceiling. In other words, she had had advice as to the modernization of those two rooms.

"She was prepared not only with instructions for the workmen, which included cutting down a marble-topped table, but she had a sample of silver-gray silk to show the men who were to decorate the dining room.

"On the twelfth of September she wrote a letter to Keene's in New York; Keene's, I may tell you, has been most obliging over long-distance telephone, consulted clerks and files on the spot, and will follow up with a letter. They were able to inform Duckett that Miss Radford's letter asked whether they could duplicate for her two rooms in their latest model house—the Pink-and-Green Parlor and the Mauve Dining room. She wanted only rugs and furniture, curtains, seats for a bench (measurements enclosed), and the wall mirror.

"They replied in the affirmative, asking a whacking deposit of course, and three weeks to a month to complete the order from their factories. She sent a money order for the deposit next day.

"Keene first mailed her an itemized list with prices,

dimensions of rugs, and colored pictures of both rooms. She O.K.'d their letter.

"Transportation difficulties held up delivery until mid-October, when the vans arrived, and with them Keene's man, Mr. Willis. Mr. Willis saw everything in its place, went into raptures over Miss Radford's vases, lamp, and wax flowers, and departed mystified. He could only assume that she was going to open a very elegant little private hotel. He came to the telephone himself to tell Duckett two things: Miss Radford had put into his hands cash amounting to more than two thousand dollars, and she had twice retired to the back parlor, certainly to consult with someone.

"Well." Gamadge leaned back in his chair, drank some whiskey, and looked at his audience. "Have you ever heard a much odder story?"

"Her money went to her head, that's all," said Fanny Hunter.

"The queerness of the story doesn't lie in the fact that she spent the money," her husband told her, "but in the kind of things she bought, and the manner in which she bought them."

"Exactly," said Gamadge. "The party in the back parlor managed to remain there during the whole transaction; yet he, or she, must have told her about Keene's rooms, perhaps showed her Keene's catalogue, got her that sample of gray silk, told her how to cut down a monstrous piece of Victorian furniture into a coffee table; must have instructed her to use the vases, the lamp and the wax flowers as she used them; must have persuaded her that there was something desirable in that charming but funny parlor. Whose playful and at that time friendly mind can it have been? Don't suggest one of the Grobys!"

"Friendly?" murmured Hunter, doubt in his tone.

"Of course friendly; last autumn all was cheerful, rosy, even gay between Miss Radford and her adviser. But—as you imply—that state of things did not last; this summer Miss Radford was horribly murdered. If, as I think, one person lurked behind all these phenomena, why the change in that person's behavior?"

"The investments went wrong," said Mrs. Star with decision.

"The investments went wrong, and Miss Radford could

not be allowed to find it out. But why the building up of the ghost legend? Well, as I maintain, to localize the murder."

"Oh, no," said Mrs. Star, lifting a white hand and waving it in a negative gesture from side to side. "To involve others; Miss Radford was made to die in the cottage so that others should be blamed."

Craye, after draining his glass, set it down. "No, Leda," he said. "The murderer couldn't be sure that she'd be hurt in that accident, or spend the night here."

Gamadge put his arms on the table, clasped his hands, and leaned forward to answer Mrs. Star: "It wasn't necessary for Miss Radford to die in this cottage," he said. "It was only necessary that she should die away from home."

Mrs. Star drew back a little from his intent look. "Away from home?"

"No doubt the time was short, no doubt the murderer seized the lucky chance that she was here, in the room her sister died in, with Clara to testify to the dress and the sunbonnet; but the murder could have taken place in the fields or on the road. For after the murder came the third and last move in that end-game—you remember? The pawn has been sacrificed, the Queen has been removed, and then comes the final sweep across the board—to the Radford farm: undefended at last, since the first thing Knapp and Hunter had to do after the accident was to wake old Sam and make him tie up the dogs."

"Ah." Hunter stretched out his legs with a sigh. "We are on solid ground at last. Gamadge, I congratulate you."

"I don't get it," said Craye.

"Don't you?" Hunter glanced at him sidewise. "The dogs had to be chained up so that people could get in and out of the farm while Alvira was out of circulation. We realized that at once. I thought we never should wake Sam."

"Well, what difference would that make to the killer?"

"All the difference, Gil;" and Craye's glance, fixed on Gamadge, flickered at the latter's tone. "Miss Radford didn't know it, but she possessed something more valuable than money to her murderer; she hadn't hidden it, I'm sure; it was probably in a pigeonhole of her desk, among bills, and old and new leases."

"Well, whatever it was, why couldn't the fellow walk in

one evening, knock her brains out, and..." he paused.

"Those dogs." Gamadge smiled. "How Miss Radford's kind adviser and friend must have raged that *they* were bought without consultation! Miss Radford could let a caller in past them, but she couldn't, if she were dead, let a caller out. Nor could a visitor very well ask her to chain them up for the duration of a visit, or risk making off with the desired object while she lived. As for the classic tradition of poisoned meat, how difficult in practice to follow! For there were two dogs; and what if one of them got the whole bait, or neither of them touched it? The trick couldn't be tried twice, since the meat would be found next morning if a dead dog wasn't, and Miss Radford put on the alert."

"But what *was* the thing the murderer wanted?" almost screamed Fanny Hunter.

"Dear Fanny, I can only think that it was something which connected the murderer with those securities. Why should Miss Radford lock it away, since she thought it harmless, and since the person implicated was her friend?"

Mrs. Star said: "Horrible." She added, after a silence, "Mr. Gamadge, I cannot but think of those Grobys. I do not like to accuse anyone; but this is only an inquiry, you have no proofs."

"None."

"They had a motive, the only motive we know; they are the persons most likely to be informed of Miss Radford's private affairs; they might have taken those securities, pretended to invest them, and sold them. They might have lost or spent the money. With Miss Radford dead, they have only to pretend that the bonds are gone. As for what you say about the decorations at the farm, I have been in this country for some years now; I am always amazed at the cleverness, the imitative qualities of American women. Even the poorest of them learn so fast, develop so much taste from the papers and moving pictures and magazines. Could not Mrs. Groby have encouraged Miss Radford to spend money at the farm in order to show interest, lack of egotism?"

Fanny said eagerly: "And Mrs. Groby probably knew all about those two dresses and sunbonnets. And Mr. Groby is such a horrid little man; he isn't even honest, is he?"

"No," said Gamadge, "his record isn't good."

Craye said: "Thumbs down on the Grobys."

"But who else is there, Gil?" asked Fanny.

"Anybody Alvira Radford knew."

"And who knew about this cottage, Mrs. Hickson's wardrobe, the condemned door, and all the rest of it." Hunter shook his head. "Not anybody, Fanny."

"And *still*," cried Fanny, "we don't know how on earth Miss Radford was killed!"

"Mrs. Gamadge fainted," said Mrs. Star. "There can be no doubt that she fainted. If she had not fainted, the murderer would have killed her, too."

Clara had sat silent and grave throughout the conference; even now she did not speak, or even shake her head.

"Well," and Gamadge picked up his typed papers and restored them to their envelope, "there we are. I am to find out who it was that persuaded Miss Radford to do her shopping at Keene's, and afterwards had an immediate and pressing need for seventy thousand dollars; not a huge sum to kill for. Meanwhile, let's have at least one rubber of bridge—it isn't late."

But it was rather late, and only one rubber was played. Fanny begged off, and so did Clara; but the game was not what it had been on the preceding night, with Craye and Mrs. Star wiping Hunter and Gamadge off the map. Craye paid no attention to the cards, and Mrs. Star was led into an injudicious double—she did not know Gamadge well enough to know that he never bid without cards.

As the others were saying good night to Clara, Hunter took Gamadge aside. He asked with a doubtful look: "Er—have you any firearms, old man?"

"No, I can't say I have."

"I can supply you tomorrow; but I'd be better pleased if you were—I think the word is heeled—tonight."

"Don't think of it. Besides, I have no license; I understand that your State is punctilious; I'd better speak to Duckett first."

"I could drive up and back in no time."

"I'd do the driving, but I really think the matter isn't pressing."

"Your exposition has made me as nervous as a cat—on your behalf. I hardly know why."

"I'm quite nervous myself."

They both laughed. The guests departed, and Clara was

about to climb the living-room stairs when Gamadge, shutting and locking the door, spoke over his shoulder: "I think we might as well try the other bedroom tonight."

"The Herons'? Maggie's in it!"

"I had a word with her before dinner, and she agreed to move back to her own room. She'll be right at the head of our stairs, you know."

"But for goddness' sake why?"

"I just thought I'd like to see what it was like."

Clara looked at his averted face, asked no questions, and went upstairs. She found that Maggie had transferred her belongings and Gamadge's, their bedding and their books, to the other room, which was cosy and cheerful with lamps and flowers. It was very snug, but Clara did not sleep well there. In the first place, Gamadge not only locked both doors, but put a chair under each knob. In the second place, she woke towards morning convinced that she heard a kind of scrabbling outside, at the north end of the cottage. Gamadge had disappeared. She looked out of the window, which seemed very high above the ground, could see nothing, and almost instantly felt Gamadge's hand on her arm.

"Nothing at all," he said, and replaced the chair beneath the knob of the door. "Squirrels on our bedroom porch."

This time Clara slept until morning.

16

The Ladder

Next morning Clara went into the north bedroom, unfastened and opened the doors and windows, and then went out and looked at the rustic stairway and porch. She was examining a scarred and broken crosspost under the little platform when Eli came sauntering down the road. He climbed the hillside to join her.

"Good morning," said Clara.

"Good morning." Eli looked at the splintered rustic bough from which bark hung in shreds; he followed Clara's glance from it to the window above and on the left.

"New break," he said.

"Yes. It must have happened last night, Eli. We heard something, but Mr. Gamadge thought it was an animal of some kind."

"It wasn't done in the storm? Tree falling?" Eli had evidently dismissed the animal with the contempt it deserved. Clara was rather glad she had not mentioned squirrels.

"I don't think it was broken yesterday," she said, "and there wasn't any fallen tree."

Eli said: "I thought you slep' in there."

"Last night we didn't."

Eli proceeded to a silent demonstration; he put a foot on a lower strut, sprang up, caught hold of the railing, and put his other foot—the left one—on a solid end of the broken bough. Then he swung away from the railing, gripped the window sill with his left hand, and peered in. The bough emitted a loud and ominous cracking sound, and he jumped lightly down to the slope below. He stood looking at Clara.

"Why didn't they go to a window on the other side of the house?" she asked him.

Eli pointed. There was a faint indication on the leaves that carpeted the slope, which might to his eyes be the trace of recent footsteps. He led the way, avoiding them, up the little hill and around the cottage to the nearer back window. Thence he looked down along the rear of the house.

"Came up this way first," he said, waving a brown hand at the long grass below. "Window shut. Came around to the front. I think they wore a skirt. You didn't hear any car?"

"No. Henry thinks they always left the car on the highway or up the reservation road—before."

Eli got his pipe and tobacco out, lighted the pipe, and replaced his tobacco in his pocket. He said: "You might have a man here."

"A watchman? I don't think Henry wants one."

Eli drifted away. Clara sat down on the doorstone, where she was joined a few minutes later by Gamadge. He had mail for her; one long, flimsy envelope contained her summons to the inquest on the body of Alvira Radford; it was to be held at Avebury Town Hall on Monday, July 13th, at ten o'clock.

"We'll be there," said Gamadge, "and so will Bob Macloud. You'll like Bob being there, won't you?"

She let him light a cigarette for her; then she said: "I'm making so much trouble for everybody. Henry—ought I to say that perhaps I did faint, after all?"

He took his cigarette out of his mouth to give her the smile she liked best, full of love, comprehension and amusement. "Say what you think."

"I can only say what I saw."

"And it will be one of the most impressive instances of direct versus circumstantial evidence on record. But a letter was once written advising its recipients to put faith in the evidence of things *not* seen; I shall obey it—you mustn't."

"They wouldn't like me to bring Saint Paul into it, would they?"

"No, hang it all, they want fact. You stick to it."

A horn sounded from the road. Gamadge went around the house to find Hunter at the wheel of his car. He leaned out and handed Gamadge a parcel.

"Here you are," he said, looking quizzical. "Fully loaded, safety catch on, and never—so far as I know—been fired in anger. My father acquired it during the last war. You'd better test its powers against a tree."

Gamadge thanked him. "I'll let Clara have a shot," he said. "She's good at pistols, which is more than I can say for myself."

"I have to tell you that poor Fanny's rather upset today."

"I'm sorry to hear that. Why?"

"Well, you sent her home last night in a thoughtful and doubting mood. Doubts at last submerged and overwhelmed her. She went to bed very unhappy, began to cry at two A.M., and had me up shortly afterwards to communicate her sorrows."

"What was the trouble?" Gamadge had unwrapped his parcel, and now weighed a rather large automatic pistol in his hand; he seemed to like the feel of it.

"Well, as you may know, Craye was invited to dine here last Saturday with Fanny and me, but declined on the score of a previous engagement."

"Yes, I know."

"Last night Mrs. Star and Fanny were in the dressing room just after dinner, and Mrs. Star casually said something which—though Fanny did not realize it at the moment—seems to mean that Craye had no previous engagement at all. He appears to have come home rather late for dinner that evening, and went up to bed early. They all live quite independently, I believe; Mrs. Star, for instance, has a car at her disposal and comes and goes as she likes.

"Well, Fanny casually passed this bit of information along to me. Then came your discourse. Fanny—after clutching eagerly at Mrs. Star's argument as to the guilt of the Grobys—began to worry very much; not, mind you, because she thinks Craye can be your man, but because she was afraid that I might casually pass the fact of his destroyed alibi on to you."

"But *your* immediate reaction to her story was to offer me a gun."

"I thought a gun could do you no harm."

"It might have come in handy last night. We had a caller; at least we heard somebody about the cottage, and this morning Eli found tracks."

"No! Really, Gamadge, this is too much. I don't know how you can expose Clara to it."

"I'd rather expose her to anything than to that inquest."

"You and she had better come back to us."

"She makes converts by staying here. Everybody is thinking up ways of exonerating her."

"Exonerating her! The thing's fantastic, and if there is lunacy in it somewhere, as I begin to believe, the lunacy isn't Clara's. Well, last night I promised Fanny that I would say no word to you about Craye and his non-alibi without her express permission, and I make no apologies for the promise; I knew that the facts, whatever they are, would sooner or later be dug up by you or Duckett or Ledwell. But this morning I am told by the invaluable Colley that neither have the Grobys any alibis for the crucial dates and hours."

"They haven't. Duckett says Groby was driving about alone on every occasion, presumably for business reasons, and that Mrs. Groby was always at home alone, with an extra car in their private garage."

"Well! Those unfortunate and dismal Grobys; who is to protect them, while people of our sort protect other people of our sort? Last night I didn't much care for the

way Mrs. Star took it upon herself to argue the case
against them; I can see now that she was probably a good
deal worried by that time at the memory of her own
indiscretion to Fanny.

"I put the case to Fanny. She is very fair-minded, and
she at last agreed to let me put it to you, on condition that
she might speak to Craye first. She shut herself up in our
telephone cupboard, and I may say that the first thing I
shall do when the war is over will be to get an extension
put in. I simply cannot communicate with people while
standing in a mummy case. I make poor Fanny do most of
the communicating. She told me that Craye said he would
call you and explain."

"He hasn't called yet."

"He will, and thanks to our warning he will explain. But
Heavens, we must be completely on the wrong track; I tell
myself so a dozen times a day. What motive could he
possibly have?"

"If people's bliss depends on a lot of money, and they're
short of money—"

"Short of money? The Crayes have been rolling ever
since Grandfather Craye went into copper mines, in the
big days."

"Or Alvira Radford might have had something on him."

"Craye has had practically everything on him since he
left school, and survived."

The telephone was heard to ring. Hunter, with a smile
and a wave of the hand, drove on; Gamadge went into the
cottage. Craye's voice came hurried over the wire:

"Gamadge?"

"Hello, Gil."

"We're all of a twitter here this morning. As far as I can
make out, Mrs. Star and Mrs. Hunter think they've let out
something about me that will land me in jail, and Mrs.
Star says that you'd see the whole human race extermi-
nated in order to save Mrs. Gamadge from a moment's
anxiety. I told her I didn't blame you."

"Clara must hear that; she'll be flattered. What's the
fuss about?"

"It seems that Mrs. Star told Mrs. Hunter last night that
I had no engagement after all for last Saturday night. I'd
refused one for dinner at the cottage, you know. Well, I
did have one; a man was coming to see me on business. I

expected him at about nine o'clock, and I didn't mention the engagement to any of my household—why should I have mentioned it? I waited for him until eleven, and then went to bed. Oh—I meant to say that I went up to bed at ten, but I have a telephone up there. He telephoned at one—his plane had been delayed. He came on Sunday."

"I see."

"He's off again now, and I'm afraid you won't be able to get in touch with him to check up—if you want to check up. I don't know why you should, but your talk last night seems to have made all the women nervous. Their minds are running on alibis and stuff. Mrs. Hunter was all upset because she'd told Hunter, and the Grobys had no alibis, and he thought they'd better tell you. I can't make head or tail of it all. Are you still convinced that I'm withholding information about the Radford woman?"

"You are."

"Nothing of any value to you, nothing at all. But if you're wasting time on me, perhaps I'd better have a talk with you—clear it all up. I would have before, but it wasn't entirely my business; in fact, I ought to consult other people first. Now what I suggest is this: I'll drive over late this afternoon, can't make it before. But I don't want to talk in your cottage; it's a bird cage, and I want to avoid shutting ourselves up as though we were talking secrets. Same goes for my place here—you saw the situation; and the wretched Medos kids crawl out of cupboards and from behind curtains. You know that trail—the Ladder?"

"Yes; I know it."

"I'll meet you up there, I'll leave my car on the road."

"Why shouldn't we talk in your car?"

"Anybody might come along. I tell you I don't want people to think we have secrets."

"Why shouldn't we have secrets?"

"I'll explain. Five o'clock?"

Gamadge, after a moment, said: "All right."

"Thanks very much." The hurry and strain left Craye's voice. He said: "I suppose I was a fool not to be more candid at first, but—oh, well; I've made up my mind now."

"Might I ask whom you're going to consult about our meeting on the Ladder?"

"Oh—well, I'd rather not say."

"Mrs. Star knows already, doesn't she?"

"Er—yes. Naturally, since we talked about my clearing the thing up."

"You wouldn't mind telling me whether you're going to consult more than one other person?"

"I don't know why you should be interested."

"I am, though."

"Only one person, in the strictest confidence."

Gamadge left the telephone, got an empty jar from the kitchen, and called Clara. They went up the road, and he fixed the jar in the crotch of a tree; Clara smashed it squarely with her first shot. Gamadge refused to use more ammunition. "I don't think," he said, "I'll improve my marksmanship with one shot—or with twenty."

"I hope we're not going to kill five people," said Clara, affecting sarcasm.

"We can't kill anybody until Duckett fixes me up with a permit."

Gamadge drove into Avebury that afternoon. When he returned he had a dip in the pool, and then dressed and strolled up the road. The pistol was in his coat pocket.

Clara called after him: "I'll bring you your stick, if you're taking a walk."

"If I want a stick, I'll pick one up."

He turned back twice to look at her before he rounded the bend.

Craye's car stood glittering just beyond the green tunnel that was the entrance to the Ladder. Gamadge left the warm brightness of the road for shade, coolness, quiet broken by the occasional crack of a twig or rustle of leaves. With his hand lightly clasping the handle of the gun, he began the ascent; the walking was even rougher than before—new channels had been washed in the soft earth by the storm of Thursday night. He balanced along the tops of the ruts, with long steps from rock to rock. The stream made itself heard on his right.

Twenty yards ahead the trail lost itself around a bend, and a solid wall of trees confronted him. It was from the corner of his eye that he caught sight of the thing half camouflaged among bushes to the right, patterned with light and shade. It was up at the very turn of the track, and he would never have seen it if he had not been on the watch; but he made out the faded purple of dress and sunbonnet. A bush or briar seemed to have plucked the dress away from the left shoulder—there was a patch of light brown where it had been. Gamadge caught a glimpse of brown flatness under the sunbonnet, like features barely evident through the last wrappings of a mummy.

The appearance was so daunting that in spite of himself Gamadge stood for an instant motionless; but as a purple arm rose, he fired. No answering shot came; he had dodged off the trail and behind a tree before he heard one, like a belated echo of his own.

Utter silence followed, and when he peeped from behind his defense the figure had vanished. He listened, heard no crackle of leaves underfoot to warn him that he was being encircled, and began a circumspect advance from tree to tree; but when he rounded the bend he stepped forth into the open; the incident seemed to be closed. A gray-brown figure lay twisted like a snake across the trail; its head was against the edge of a rock, its raised left shoulder dripped with blood. At its feet lay a sordid heap of purple garments, torn off and flung down in an abandonment of wild haste. An automatic pistol showed among the limp folds of the sunbonnet; its barrel was warm to the touch of Gamadge's fingers.

17

No More Disguise

Eli came crashing through the woods on the right. He stopped in his stride at the edge of the trail, and like a wild creature at gaze took in the scene before him.

"You did stick around, then. Good for you." Gamadge had his handkerchief out, and was searching Craye's pocket for another. Eli, his clasp knife already in his hand, turned his black eyes from the automatic in Gamadge's left hand to the one that lay among folds of purple calico. "Did he git *you?*"

"No." Gamadge lifted Craye, while Eli cut pale fawn-colored shirting from the wounded shoulder. Eli said: "You got him, all right. Bullet went right through. Pad him up before he bleeds to death."

They padded up both wounds with the handkerchiefs, strips of Craye's shirt, and a staying outer bandage of Eli's far from antiseptic bandanna. Gamadge meanwhile described the occurrences of the past ten minutes. "His car's just down the road," he ended.

"We'll take him to Stratfield Hospital. Is it Mr. Craye?"

"Yes."

Eli examined the back of Craye's head. "He won't die of your shot, but he got an awful bang on that rock when he fell."

"Take charge of this, will you?" Gamadge had replaced his gun in his pocket; he lifted the other by its barrel, shifted the safety catch, and handed it to Eli. Eli said: "It's a .38 too."

"So I see. It was fired from over here, but I can't see the shell." Gamadge hunted about on the extreme edge of the trail.

"Could be in the stream, beyond or back of you. I wouldn't want the job of finding it, or finding your bullet, either."

"Nor I."

Eli picked up purple calico, a pair of brown silk gloves, and a strip of brown chiffon veiling. He stuffed the latter articles in his pocket, hung the sunbonnet over his arm, and shook out the draggled and spattered dress. "Where's the bullet hole?"

"Oh. The dress was pulled away from the fellow's shoulder; I saw a lightish-brown patch."

"An' fired at it. Bull's eye." Eli showed Gamadge how to make a stretcher of their coats, and how to get Craye on it. "Mustn't shake him up." Eli bundled the purple dress, and placed it under the injured head. "Might be a concussion, looks that way to me."

They went carefully down the trail. Eli said: "He thought first he wasn't hurt so bad, got out of the clothes and perhaps dropped the gun on purpose. But he bled too much, fainted in his tracks, went down bang on that rock. Was you watchin' for him?"

"You bet I was watching; but I thought I'd get shot as I jumped for a tree on the other side of the trail."

"Perhaps he didn't know you had a gun; surprised him a second. Then he took one shot at you, and decided he'd better get out of here."

They soon reached the road. Craye was got into the back of his car, with Eli beside him to steady him against jolts; but there were no jolts. Gamadge, relying on Eli's first aid work, drove with more care than speed.

The moment Craye was out of his charge and in the hands of the orderlies at Stratfield hospital, Gamadge made for a telephone.

"Don't wait dinner," he told Clara. "I'm stuck in Stratfield for I don't know how long."

"How on earth did you get to Stratfield? Walk?"

"I got here in Craye's car. He—er—had an accident."

"Right up there on the road?"

"Right up there. I'm at Stratfield hospital. You and Maggie will be all right till I get back; the case is busted, Clara."

"Oh, Henry, what on earth—"

"I'll tell you when I see you. You won't be the star witness at the inquest, I will."

"May I tell the Hunters? Perhaps they'll come down and have supper."

"Good idea. Yes, tell them. No reason why not."

When he turned away from the telephone Ledwell was behind him, eyes snapping. "Well, I understand you broke the case for us, Mr. Gamadge; glad of it, of course; but this is a terrible thing for Stratfield. Terrible. Our best old family. I understand—Eli says Craye called you up and asked you to meet him in the woods. Wanted to give you private information."

"Yes."

"But you took your gun along. Why? Had it doped out that he was the killer?"

"I knew he had the idea from something I said last night that I was on the warpath."

"You saw him start to shoot, fired first, and got him in the shoulder. When you reached the bend he'd just had time to strip off the dress and sunbonnet, but he fainted before he could fire again. He could have said later that somebody wearing the clothes had got both of you."

"So he could."

"We've been working on those Jeans women since

yesterday, and I think we'll come out all right on the
motive for the Radford killing. We can put them on the
stand to swear that they got some scandal about him and
that refugee—Mrs. Star, she calls herself—from Alvira
Radford. They can testify, it isn't hearsay, because Craye's
relations with the Star woman aren't the issue; the issue is
whether the story was circulated, whether he heard about
it, and whether it tended to incite him to murder. Can you
help us on that? I mean, have you any evidence tending to
show that he'd heard the story?"

"My wife could repeat a conversation she had with him,
but I'm not sure that a jury would be allowed to infer
anything from it."

"We'll work on that; what I'm hoping is that he'll come
through himself. We're getting Mrs. Star over here, and
we'll have her in the room when he comes to—if he does.
The doctor won't promise anything for tonight. We'll have
her here, though; we might get some information from
what they say to each other."

"I don't think Mrs. Star will oblige you with much
information."

"Not if she's an accomplice. Anyhow, we'll keep her
here; we don't want those refugees cooking up a lot of
alibis for Craye. I only hope they haven't cooked any up
already; for last Saturday, I mean."

"They haven't. One of the things that gave him the
jitters was the fact that Mrs. Star spoiled his Saturday
alibis last night."

"No! That's something anyhow. His man's gone, half his
help are gone, and he could go in and out, make all the
trips he pleased, nobody the wiser. We know that. I never
could see the Grobys in all this; couldn't see them thinking
up that circus with Mrs. Hickson's old clothes."

"But there's the financial end of it to consider, Ledwell,
isn't there? Those lost securities of Alvira Radford's."

Ledwell, fiddling with his hat, frowned. "We don't know
they're lost. They may turn up. She may have been selling
'em one by one, living on the proceeds. You can't tell what
an elderly woman will get into her head in times like
these. But you also can't tell what happens to big fortunes
in times like these. Craye might have been short of cash,
funnier things have happened. He's paying terrific alimony
to that wife of his, but they say she's tough, with a tough

background—she may have something on him. Even the Craye fortune couldn't stand up against steady blackmail."

"No."

"Terrible job, though, looking into these rich men's financial affairs; they're protected by all sorts of buffers and dummies."

"I'll have the name of an investigator tomorrow; I was thinking of employing him myself. And I could let you have my notes on the case. Perhaps by tomorrow I may have fresh ideas on the subject."

"I hope so." Ledwell looked eager. "And I want you to let me send you home in my car. I appreciate your work on this case, Mr. Gamadge, and I appreciate the way you're coöperating. I want to say I'm glad the thing's breaking the way it is."

"So am I."

An orderly put his head into the waiting room, to say that a woman called Star was making a fuss in the office.

"Send her up to me." Ledwell posed sternly beside a table with a potted palm on it, until—a few seconds later—Mrs. Star stood in the doorway. Her long gray cloak gave her a military air, and her bare head was also soldierly—rigid on her neck. She looked like one who is no stranger to official interference. She ignored Gamadge.

"I demand to know," she said, "what has happened to Mr. Craye. I was told that he had had an accident; but when I arrive I am not allowed to see him, and I am given no information. I am told by an officer of the state police that I am not to go back and talk to Mr. Medos and Madame Fouret."

"Don't you want to wait till he's conscious, Mrs. Star?" Ledwell returned her stony gaze stonily.

"I wish to be free to come and go. Was Mr. Craye attacked?"

"I don't know why you should think so."

"You are at war."

"I haven't heard of anybody being attacked because they harbored refugees."

"Have you not?"

"No," said Ledwell, "and neither have you."

"You don't know all that can happen when a country is at war with the Axis powers." She turned her head stiffly to look at Gamadge. "What has this gentleman," she asked, "to do with Mr. Craye's accident?"

Gamadge said equably: "I was on the spot. I found Mr. Craye on the Ladder trail, just above the cottage, knocked out."

Mrs. Star did not exactly stagger, but she certainly stepped backwards as if she had lost her balance. She said, recovering herself, "Knocked out?" and suddenly there were tears in her eyes.

"From a fall," Ledwell ammended, but she paid no attention.

"Mr. Craye has been our best friend," she said. "He means a great deal to the people in his house. Is he seriously hurt?"

"Every chance of his getting over it," Ledwell told her.

"I should like to go and tell Mr. Medos and Madame Fouret that. Then I shall return."

"The truth is, Mrs. Star, we don't want his accident talked about till he wakes up and tells us about it himself."

"Then you do know that it was an attack! And I am to be kept incommunicado until you get evidence. Is there no law in your country in wartime?"

Ledwell, irritated, remarked that she seemed to have the war on the brain.

She answered him more quietly: "It is true; I have. I don't like the feeling—that I am not free to come and go."

"It's just that we want you to coöperate."

Mrs. Star looked as if she did not at all wish to coöperate. She said: "That is jargon."

"It's what?"

"Jargon."

Ledwell, outraged by this brutal assault on his well-loved vocabularly, looked furious. Gamadge said: "Perhaps you have not been quite frank with Mr. Ledwell, Mrs. Star; let him have the privilege of being not quite frank with you. And remember that if you leave the hospital now you may not get into it again; perhaps there are others who have a closer claim to be with Gilbert Craye while he is here."

She gazed at him silently.

"Let them put you in a comfortable visitors' room," continued Gamadge. "They'll bring you something to eat.

They'll let you know the moment Craye is able to see anyone."

She said: "Do you know why I hesitate to put faith in your advice, Mr. Gamadge? I think you would stop at nothing to clear your wife of blame in this Radford affair. I think you would like to fasten blame on anyone else."

"Now listen!" Ledwell was shocked. "We never had any idea of suspecting Mrs. Gamadge of any motive for the murder."

"No; but she was there in that room when Miss Radford was killed, and those clothes of Mrs. Hickson's were in the cottage; both sets of them. They must have been. But she cannot be guilty. I will tell you who can, in your opinion— an enemy alien."

"If she has a motive," said Ledwell, shortly.

"Motive? You will find me a motive."

Ledwell, still more shocked, protested without rancor: "You've evidently had your mind completely warped by your experiences in your own country. Let me tell you that in our courts the prosecution doesn't have to show motive; we only need evidence. Nobody's accusing you of anything. We merely don't want you rushing back and forth between Craye's and the hospital, making talk. I'll go get somebody to show you a place to wait."

He departed. Mrs. Star, her eyes fixed on Gamadge— and there was, he thought, a baleful light in them—said coldly: "Last night, Mr. Gamadge, you were making a case against someone in that living room of yours. You were making it out against Mr. Craye, because through my fault you thought he had offered a false alibi for last Saturday night. Through my fault. Today he goes to explain to you privately, and tonight he is lying injured in this hospital."

"He told you that he was coming to meet me on the Ladder?"

"Of course he told me."

"Only you?" Gamadge's expression was so odd that her own changed. She said with sudden contempt: "I suppose you do not imagine that *I* would hurt him!"

"You seem to have your own ideas as to who hurt him."

A hospital aide in a smock came smiling in, and invited Mrs. Star to come upstairs. Mrs. Star, without another look at Gamadge, followed her into the corridor.

Ledwell hurried back. "They won't let him see anybody

tonight," he said, "even if he should come to. It's a concussion, all right. I'd like to send that wildcat back home."

"If you try to, you'll have another battle. She won't budge now."

"My idea is that she's in a panic."

"Several kinds of panic. I must be going, Ledwell."

Ledwell saw him to the car, and lingered at its window as though grudging the departure of so useful a deputy. "You don't mind if we keep that gun of yours till after the inquest?" he inquired.

"Not a bit. Hunter lent it to me; I'll tell him it's an exhibit."

"Craye's is a .38 too. There isn't a mark on it—he had the number filed off. If you hadn't got him through a big blood vessel you'd be dead now, and the whole thing a worse mystery than ever. You seem to know how to take pretty good care of yourself, Mr. Gamadge, but in these matters it's just as well to confide in the law. We could have had a couple of men there."

"I'm afraid that if there had been a couple of men, there wouldn't have been any evidence."

"Well, you can take care of yourself. Of your wife, too. Remember me to her. I'd like to meet her again."

"You must come around some day."

"When I saw that cottage on Sunday, I thought I'd have the horrors in it."

"It's much more cheerful now."

Gamadge asked the plain-clothes driver of Ledwell's car to stop at the telegraph office. He sent a seven word telegram to Macloud, and then had himself driven home.

18

Quite Safe Now

When he arrived at the cottage Clara and Fanny Hunter burst from the dining-room doorway to batter him with questions; Clara had him by one arm, Fanny by the other, and Hunter, in the background, vainly tried to make himself heard. At last he succeeded: "Let the man come in and get something to eat. He must be famished."

"We have your dinner waiting," Clara told him. "We've only just finished coffee. It's only nine."

"Well, I'll eat the dinner," said Gamadge, "but Hunter must keep me company."

"We'll all keep you company!" Fanny shook his arm. "We want to know what happened to poor Gilbert Craye."

"He's getting along very well. You can't watch me eat dinner, Fanny, because you and Clara must move things back into the north bedroom."

"Oh, can we go back?" Clara's face brightened.

"Of course we can go back; didn't I tell you the case is all washed up? We shall be quite safe now."

"But does that mean—oh!" Fanny dropped his arm, and backed away. "Oh, Henry, it can't mean that Gil Craye killed Miss Radford!"

"I'll talk it over first with your husband. I need counsel and encouragement."

Hunter said: "You two had really better go upstairs for a while. I'll see that Gamadge gets his dinner."

But Clara saw that he got his dinner. Then, leaving him to the company of his male guest, she took Fanny up by the enclosed stair. Gamadge provided Hunter with ice, whiskey, a tumbler and a siphon; but after pouring himself coffee, he rose, shut the dining-room door and the stairway door, and returned to his seat at the end of the narrow table.

"I want to tell you the whole story," he said, "and then we can edit it. It's not for women's ears—it's a tale of Indians, shooting, villainy unmasked and buckets of gore."

"Don't tell me that you actually had to use that ammunition I provided you with!"

"Didn't I, though."

"Is Craye mad?"

"You shall judge. He's at present in Stratfield hospital with concussion and a bullet wound in his shoulder."

"Good Lord. I'm glad you escaped without damage."

"I escaped by something as near a miracle as anything that's not a miracle can be." Gamadge retold his story; the ascent of the trail, the purple figure among the trees, his shot, the delayed answering shot, and the discovery of

Craye and the discarded habiliments of Mrs. Hickson's ghost.

Hunter, his expression at first incredulous and then blank, pushed his chair back from the table, crossed his legs, and sat as one stunned, until Gamadge had completed the story with an account of events at the hospital. Then he said: "No, I refuse to allow Craye's refugees a part in this wild tale. It's too much. Am I to believe that he has been harboring a nest of secret agents, or is involved in counterespionage? What am I to believe? Has he thrown everything to the winds for the sake of the beautiful spy of fiction, who has designs on the Stratfield defense plans?"

"Well, we must admit that Mrs. Star isn't exactly an ordinary kind of refugee."

"All his refugees have always been oddities. But to kill a farm woman like Alvira Radford for seventy thousand dollars—to have needed seventy thousand dollars badly enough for that—it does sound as though someone or some organization must have been bleeding him."

"Well, as Ledwell says, the prosecution won't have to show motive if it can produce evidence; but the trouble is, can it?"

"Won't the discovery of those Hickson rags and that—ugh—that veil and those gloves—be evidence enough?"

"That he wore them; yes, it might be."

"Might be?"

"If it weren't for *my* evidence."

"Yours?"

"That's what I wanted to discuss. I shall have to get up on the witness stand and swear that it wasn't I who shot Gilbert Craye."

"It wasn't you? I thought you said—"

"I fired, but I fired wide."

"My dear man! I am an enemy to the use of coincidence when coincidence can be avoided. Who else was taking potshots at him, and who else managed to hit him on the one exposed spot he offered you? You say there was no bullet hole in the Hickson dress."

"I couldn't possibly have hit that exposed spot. I took good care not to hit that figure in the purple dress. The last thing I wanted was to hit it. I'm not a marksman, and I might have killed the fellow. I wanted him to survive, and be able to furnish evidence which should forever clear my wife of involvement in the Radford murder."

Hunter's cigarette had been sending a blue stream of smoke straight into the air. Now he laid the cigarette down. "I don't understand this at all," he said. "Who else can have known that Craye was to meet you on the Ladder trail?"

"Well, he had told Mrs. Star."

"Had he, indeed?" Hunter picked up his cigarette again and smoked thoughtfully. Then he said: "No, absurd. There cannot have been two shots fired at Craye. You're simply a worse marksman than you think you are, Gamadge; you aim at the barn door, and you shoot out the lock."

"I didn't even aim at the barn door. I aimed at the barnyard."

"Then we must think of some other explanation for Craye's wound. Some person expected you both to come up the trail, but expected you to come together. How will that do?"

"Very well, I think."

"But Craye came first."

"And had to be disposed of, but not by a bullet."

"Why not?"

"Because I should have heard the shot. So he was knocked out, and deposited with his head against the rock. Knocked out from behind, you know—when he does come to, he won't be able to tell what hit him."

"Good Heavens." Hunter was silent for a few moments. Then he said: "And what about that corner of tan shirt you saw when the figure stood among the trees waiting for you? Must we have a coincidence after all, or did the murderer buy himself a shirt, hoping that Craye would be kind enough to wear one of the same color on this occasion? By Jove, that does sound a little as if the plot had originated in his own household, doesn't it?"

"Yes. But Craye always does wear that combination of gray-browns in the country; at least, Clara says he wore it on Friday of last week, and he wore it when I saw him on Thursday at his place. However, I don't think the spectre in the woods had acquired a shirt of Craye's preferred shade; I think the patch I saw on its shoulder was a patch of skin."

"Skin?"

"Skin, with a healthy tan on it."

"Excellent guess. Well, then: Craye, who was presumably waiting for you, comfortably seated on a rock, is knocked out and temporarily abandoned. Why? Because you are heard on the trail. You arrive, you are in sight, you see the figure among the trees; but the figure doesn't open fire; waits to be shot at."

"Yes," said Gamadge, smiling. "That's where the miracle came in."

"The miracle?"

"A miracle of fast thinking. The killer had not followed my mental processes, he didn't know that I should be watching for him, or expecting him to be in the Hickson disguise. He thought himself invisible behind twigs and leaves, in a shifting confusion of light and shade. But I saw him, and I fired; and in that moment, realizing that a briar had exposed his left shoulder, he changed his original plan. He had meant to kill Craye and me, plant the Hickson disguise and the unidentifiable pistol on Craye, and leave us to be discovered; I, Craye's last victim, with my borrowed and useless weapon in my hand, and Craye—the murderer and suicide.

"But how much more convincing if we were found alive, with me as a witness against him! There was plenty of time to work the trick; I wasn't going to rush the hill, and when I reached the bend I should be stopped there at sight of Craye bleeding in the road. The killer withdrew a step or so around the turn, tore off the disguise, knelt to fire through Craye's left shoulder, made sure that the bullet had gone into the woods, and vanished up the trail. Who would search for bullets, when I myself could bear witness to the source of them?

"But again I had failed to play my predestined part; I had fired wide."

Hunter, listening in fascination, asked: "Why didn't you tell all this to Ledwell?"

"I wanted to discuss it first with you. Ledwell can't proceed against Craye tonight, and Mrs. Star is immobilized in the hospital."

"I thought, by your use of the masculine pronoun throughout, that you must have eliminated her from consideration."

"I don't have to remind you of the circumlocutions imposed on us by the pronoun."

"Did it seem to you that she was abnormally anxious to get back to her friends at the Craye house?"

"She wasn't in a normal state of mind, certainly. She was greatly upset at the idea that she might be under surveillance."

"The trouble is, Gamadge: if she wanted to prevent Craye from telling you something, why didn't she kill him? And why should she at any time think it necessary to kill you?"

"I think Mrs. Star would be strongly tempted to kill anybody who showed signs of wishing to investigate her or her fellow refugees too closely; and she'd be strongly tempted to kill even Craye, fond as she is of him, if he showed signs of giving her or them away. That he wasn't killed does, as you imply, seem to let her out."

"Fond of him? How exactly do you mean that?" Hunter looked surprised.

"She loves him."

"No!"

"Under the frightful stress and uncertainty of an hour ago she couldn't conceal it."

"I shouldn't have thought—good Heavens!" Hunter was perplexed. "Two people more mutually indifferent I should have said I had never seen!"

"Craye doesn't reciprocate."

"Perhaps—no, it can't be a crime of jealousy; because one must somehow work in those wretched lost securities."

"And Miss Radford's sudden passion for paying her way in cash, and those remarkable improvements at the farm."

"At least we needn't follow Mrs. Star's kind advice and consider Mrs. Groby. Mrs. Groby wasn't on the Ladder trail this afternoon, I think you'll agree!"

"No." Gamadge returned his smile. "I can't see the genteel Mrs. Groby lying in wait for two men with a pistol, or having that inspiration and shooting Craye through the shoulder."

"Then we must consider the women in the case out of it." Hunter took a drink of whiskey, set his glass down, and suddenly looked up at Gamadge with an expression of such fierce anger that his face was the face of an unknown. "Out of it," he repeated.

Steps sounded on the enclosed stairway, and Fanny's

voice, raised in laughter, came down to them. Hunter got up and swung open the door.

"Fanny," he said.

"Yes, Phin?"

"Don't come down yet. Gamadge and I have business."

"All right. When you want us we'll be up here in the sitting room."

Hunter closed the door. Then he turned, came back to the table, and said coldly: "I'd like your conclusions, if you've come to any."

"You're welcome to them; have another drink, and make yourself comfortable."

Hunter stood for another ten seconds looking at his host; then, still frowning a little, he resumed his seat. Gamadge mixed him a highball.

"I don't know where I got the insane idea that you were about to make a fool of yourself," he said. "I apologize for it."

"You got it by an unconscious exercise in elimination; and you must have had your own reasons, Hunter, for thinking that I would think such a thing. Later I may tell you what they were; but first I should like to put my conclusions, as you call them, into the form of a story. I shall welcome suggestions or criticism."

Hunter said tranquilly: "I dare say I shan't interrupt you at all." He had regained his usual calm of manner, but he had had a shock. At a sound from above his head turned, his dark eyes were raised to the ceiling. But the sound ceased, and he relaxed in his chair.

"I begin my story," said Gamadge, after lighting a fresh cigarette, "in the summer of 1941. Mrs. Hickson is dead, Miss Radford has inherited her property, Miss Radford has discovered to her annoyance and dismay that instead of more than a hundred thousand dollars she will have a mere seventy thousand, in bonds that pay only two or three per cent a year. To Miss Radford's type all taxation seems robbery, and we may I think be certain that she is in a state of righteous indignation.

"But one day, on some shady road, as she drives along in her car or her buggy, she meets someone whom all her life she has admired and respected from afar; someone whose family has always represented distinction to Miss Radford, honor, wealth, and the highest form of civilization. Someone whom she would not hesitate to trust. This person flatters her by showing an interest in her affairs, by congratulating her on her inheritance, by sympathizing deeply with her at the loss of thirty thousand dollars to a ravening government. She listens to this person as she would not listen to her nearest relative, to the bank, to her best friend. She is delighted to hear that she can easily make up the lost thirty thousand by reinvestment in something just as safe and twice as good.

"And she is glad to leave the transaction in the hands of this kind friend, who knows all about money. She is only too quick to believe that if a word of the reinvestment gets out, the tax collectors will be down on her again. She is maliciously pleased to keep her affairs a secret.

"And she is tempted in another way; her adviser reminds her that now she will no longer be an obscure farm woman, and that she ought to take her place in the social world—not the little world of Avebury and the Grobys, but the larger one of fine houses and country estates into which her friend will introduce her when she is ready to entertain largely. I suppose that the months during which Miss Radford, guided by her friend, carried out the decorations at the farm were the happiest of her life.

"For they both enjoyed it; they were on the pleasantest terms; no doubt her kind adviser felt grateful to the woman who was saving him from ruin, and whom he fully intended to repay. That he never could repay her, that he found himself suddenly, overnight perhaps, unable to repay her, brings us to his own story and to a consideration of his own character.

"Let us say that he—like the rest of us—had been reduced to a narrower scale of living than he had known in the past, and that he had recently gone into some scheme—quite legitimate, entirely commendable, I have no doubt—and backed it with all his capital and all his credit; some scheme, perhaps an invention as tremendous as rayon or cellophane, which needed by the summer of 1941 some not very great extra supply of capital; say that he had been called upon for a hundred thousand dollars.

"And say that he hadn't a hundred thousand, had only half of that; say that he couldn't raise a penny more, and was certain, for the lack of more, to lose all. He heard of

Miss Radford's legacy, and he saw an opportunity to save himself at nobody's expense; for when he made his own fortune, within a short time now, he would not only return her seventy thousand dollars, but return it in the better-paying investments that he promised her. Meanwhile he would pay her her doubled income in cash.

"Miss Radford withdrew her securities from the Stratfield bank, and he gave her a receipt for them. He immediately turned them into cash, and turned the cash into his enterprise. And then, on the seventh of December, came the war."

Gamadge drank some of his highball, and went on:

"In a single day the legitimate enterprise was as if it had never been. Whatever material was required for it—rubber, tin, chemicals—had ceased overnight to exist for private use. And although our friend was by no means reduced to beggary, although he might by liquidating his assets have repaid Miss Radford her seventy thousand, and still had enough to live on comfortably enough, he couldn't face the prospect. Nor could he kill himself, nor could he run away; he preferred murder; because he had a wife."

Hunter looked up from his clasped hands to Gamadge's face. "Let's drop this ridiculous pretense," he said. "We're not children. Admit that you actually think you're talking about me."

19

What Money Can Buy

In the mild light of the candles the two men seemed to confront each other almost placidly; each had a dark open doorway behind him, though Hunter's back was to the mystery of the outer world, Gamadge's to that of the little green room where Alvira Radford had died. The low boom of the waterfall went ceaselessly on as they talked in subdued voices.

"I prefer the direct method myself," said Gamadge, "but I was afraid that if I began with an accusation you would take Fanny and leave the house. I wanted you to hear me through, and I had no way of keeping you except by exciting your interest. I had to leave the gun you gave me in Stratfield; your other one, the one with the numbers filed away, is of course an exhibit too. Perhaps you have a third?"

Hunter said: "I have no pistol; but I warn you, Gamadge, that if in desperation at losing your suspect you attempt to drag my private life and Fanny's into this, I shall find other means of punishing you. Not that your wild conjectures won't be laughed at—and by Ledwell first of all."

Gamadge replied: "We may as well waive the preliminaries. We both know that if you have not been suspected it is because you are considered above and beyond suspicion; the moment I tell Duckett or Ledwell that you killed Alvira Radford they'll see it for themselves; they'll investigate you, and though they may never connect you with the Radford securities, they'll discover your financial standing and activities, and they'll discover your motive."

Hunter said: "They may still require some details—the method of the murder, you know."

Few persons ever heard contempt in Gamadge's voice; Hunter heard it now, acid and unrepressed: "Method! The moment Clara told me her story on Wednesday morning I knew that you were the murderer, and all the details of that despicable crime. I left your house; and I was only sorry that the amenities had to be preserved while I tried to find immediate evidence for these local authorities who respect you so blindly. I needed none for myself—there was only one way for the murder to have been committed, and that's the way it therefore was committed."

"Perhaps you'll condescend to enlighten me, though, since I persist in declaring myself in the dark?"

"Certainly, if you prefer to waste time. At a little before twenty minutes to one last Sunday morning you took the screen out of your bedroom window, climbed through it, put on the Hickson disguise—I don't wonder that the memory of it made you shudder a few minutes ago—and walked along the back of the house and around to the condemned door in that room behind me. You had had plenty of opportunity during the remodeling of the cottage to find out that it was not sealed, but only locked; you had loosened the plug so that it would fall into the room at a touch, and you had borrowed one of the house keys. You pushed the door open, and stood there only long enough for Clara to get a good look at you; then you were around the corner and back in your room—before she had even managed to get to the doorway and to call for help.

"You answered the call. You told her that Alvira Radford was dead. But she wasn't dead, she was quietly sleeping under morphia; you never allowed Clara to approach the bed again, you didn't allow anyone else to come into the room. You got the women upstairs, you telephoned, and then you came back—" Gamadge half turned, and glanced at the black rectangle of doorway behind him—"and committed your murder at leisure and in your own way."

"That's the story you have prepared for Ledwell?" Hunter looked no more than mildly interested.

"There's a little more of it."

"Oh—yes. I had forgotten. My burglarious entry into the farm in search of mysterious papers."

"It wasn't burglary, and it took place, of course, on your way back from Avebury with Knapp's filled prescriptions. It wasn't burglary, because—since the farm wasn't broken into—you must have had a key. Little has been said about Miss Radford's purse or bag, but she had one, and it must have been somewhere about the cottage, retrieved after her accident."

"As a matter of fact, if you need facts—you don't seem to—I retrieved it myself from among the débris of the funeral flowers."

"I have no doubt there was a house key in it."

"And what mysterious papers did I abstract?"

"The receipt for the securities."

"And it was I who made those special trips up from New York last fall, to help Alvira with the decorations here and at the farm?"

"And to persuade her that she was going to enjoy a fuller and a richer life. It was safe enough for you to make promises; you fully intended to reinvest her capital, and return the new securities to her; if you failed to improve her social standing, how could she protest effectively to you, or protest at all to others? She would have been laughed at for a fool."

"And I got the Hickson clothes out of the attic while Clara and Maggie were otherwise, and built up the ghost story to keep suspicion from floating out of this neighborhood and up the mountain?"

"And came down the mountain last night to try for a potshot at me through a bedroom window. I had talked as if I were likely to investigate too widely and too deeply for your safety. You gave me a gun to cover yourself; you thought Craye and I would be together on the trail, and that I would be watching him, not for a woman in a sunbonnet. The Hickson clothes, which were to be planted on Craye, you wore once again as a disguise, if disguise were needed; and your sudden later inspiration, after I fired, was as brilliant a piece of hair-trigger judgment as I ever heard of."

"And with Craye eliminated by me, who was left to take his place as a suspect?"

"There remained four available suspects; Clara, the Grobys, Mrs. Star. You still banked on the insanity verdict against Clara, but high as your hopes in that direction were, you had at all costs to conceal them from me. You talk of leaving Fanny out of it?" Gamadge's smile was less a smile than a twisting of the lips. "You didn't leave Clara out of it, did you? It's not your fault that she's in her right senses, or that I'm alive to fight for her. But I am kinder to you than you have been to me; Fanny can't be left out of the argument, since she's the innocent cause of it all; but she can be left out of the case. Why, if not to keep her out of it, have I delayed justice and allowed Craye to remain under suspicion for even these few hours? Not, I assure you, to give you a friendly warning, Hunter; but to give you time to remove all traces of that tapped telephone wire."

As Hunter said nothing, but continued to look at him with a kind of rigid impassivity, he went on:

"You must have tapped your telephone, or how should you have known that Craye and I were meeting this afternoon on the Ladder? Fanny cannot have told you; if she had known that you were aware of our proposed conference there, you would never have dared to go there yourself for purposes of murder."

Hunter said stiffly: "Why should I have tapped our telephone?"

"To listen in on Fanny's talks with Craye. Alvira Radford had told you that they were meeting privately, I suppose in the course of Fanny's hospital trips to and from Stratfield.

Alvira would not spread the story after having done her duty by you, but she could not resist hinting at Craye's affair with a blond married woman. Her friends in Stratfield misinterpreted the hints; they thought she referred not to Fanny, but to the Baroness von Stermi. But I could see that Craye was indifferent to the unearthly charms of his refugee. Since the gossip spread he has been in agony. He was afraid that Fanny would hear the gossip, know it applied to herself, and drop him; or that you would hear of it and take it out on her. I don't think she has heard of it; but it was because she felt your unexpressed jealousy that she didn't tell you she was seeing Craye alone; and I may say that that jealousy most abominably obscured your judgment. Otherwise you would never have allowed yourself to recite that malice-inspired couplet, for Craye is not only an intelligent man, but a man of feeling. It was that couplet that betrayed your jealousy to me."

Hunter said: "Heroic fellow, Craye, no doubt."

"There are potentialities of heroism in him. He would almost rather have died than mention the gossip to me, but he was coming to confide it to me this afternoon in order to preserve, as he thought, the best interests of his refugees. But your conduct has fallen short of heroism; you were afraid that Fanny couldn't face comparative poverty with you; you were afraid of losing her to Craye, who worships her, and is a very rich man. Your happiness was more important to you than hers, than the lives of others; and I'm sure that in you I have met the supreme egotist at last."

Hunter slowly rose; supporting himself with his hands on the edge of the table, he said with a half smile: "But I'm to be a hero now, it seems; and it seems that you don't imagine yourself to be running any risk in confiding these matters to me."

"You would hardly have another try at me with three people, one of them Fanny, in the house; but perhaps I'd better warn you that it would do you no good. I sent a telegram to Macloud tonight, informing him quite openly that you are his man."

"In that case I'd better go—now. I'll call Fanny."

"Leave her with us, Hunter."

"Surely you don't imagine that I mean to—er—take her away with me? I shall merely drive her home."

"Leave her here. She'll be best with Clara."

"What, no farewells? No last word with the cause of all my woe?" He stood, swaying a little, and then said in a tone of one who argues a simple and self-evident question: "You don't quite realize what my position was, Gamadge. You don't quite understand. That thing I was backing—it was only held up for a few years, until after the war. It would have made me a fortune. But meanwhile I couldn't go on paying the Radford woman the annual four thousand I promised her, and I didn't think Fanny would be able to stand—er—adversity. Of course she is loyal, but she doesn't— never did love me. Well, I'll say good-bye. Look after her."

He went out into the dark; Gamadge saw the glow of his cigarette, and then heard him start the big car and drive away.

Clara and Fanny Hunter were sitting on the sofa upstairs, chatting in a lively manner. At sight of Gamadge, Fanny sprang up: "Are you going?" Her bright earrings twinkled like dragonflies.

"Hunter is called away."

"Without me?" she looked frightened.

"He wants you to stay with us tonight. I have bad news, Fanny; Clara, stand by."

20

Gamadge Hears Laughter

Gilbert Craye, his left arm in a sling and his freckles startling on the pallor of his smiling face, waved a greeting as Madame Fouret ushered two guests into the big bedroom. He sat up against pillows in his ancestral four-poster, at the foot of which one of the Medos children sat cross-legged, reading aloud to him in a penetrating treble. The other child crawled on the floor; it had made a train out of tortoise-shell toilet articles, and was supplying appropriate noises.

"Gamadge, hello." Craye made himself heard with some effort. "That Mr. Macloud? Hello. Come in and sit down.

Madame Fouret, will you get these gnomes out of here?"

"Ow, they're always so 'appy with you, Mr. Crye."

"All I ask is, get them out of this."

Madame Fouret got them out and closed the door. Gamadge and Macloud took chairs, and Macloud remarked that it was quite evident the Medos children belonged to an Underground Movement; they looked as though they had lived underground most of their lives.

"They practically have, poor little devils. I never know which is the girl and which is the boy. Did you notice poor old Fouret? You wouldn't believe it, but she's one of the best agents we have; she's got wonderful contacts in France, through her husband. Her name isn't Fouret, of course."

"And Mr. Medos isn't really Mr. Medos?"

"Of course not. He's invaluable. Absolutely trusted by our friends in six countries."

"Mrs. Star's family is interned, I believe?"

"And von Stermi wouldn't lift a finger. He and she have been separated for years."

Gamadge said: "I rather thought, from her reactions on Saturday evening at the hospital, that she must have faced a tribunal at some time."

"Yes, and got off by the skin of her teeth. She's rather hipped on the subject of espionage, naturally, poor thing, and she was convinced that enemy agents had got on our trail, and that I was the first victim of a general massacre. Besides, they're always terrified on account of the people they've left behind them in Europe. They'll all have to be moving on pretty soon—doesn't do for them to stay in one place too long. People get to talking. I hope that when my new lot comes there won't be any juniors, though."

Gamadge said: "I suppose when you mentioned Schenck to Clara a fortnight ago that you were trying to find out whether he'd told us about your underground agency."

"He wanted to tell you, and so did I, when you got home. I thought if Mrs. Gamadge knew, she might have a better impression of Leda Star. Get along better with her. She's a good sort, but being so jittery makes her seem stiff; she's had to repress her feelings too much."

"I'm sure," said Gamadge.

"But I'd sworn not to reveal anything without her permission. Leda finally let me call you up on Saturday and arrange that rendezvous; sporting of her, but she thought you were out for my blood, and I'd made up my mind I'd better tell you that Alvira Radford had seen Fanny and me together a couple of times, and spread some kind of story. It got to me, and I was afraid it would get to Fanny. I suppose you've told Macloud all about everything?" He turned his thin face from Gamadge to Macloud. That gentleman's saturnine face remained serious, even glum. He said: "I know all."

"Well, I'd better explain—from Fanny's and my point of view. It's all because Fanny's so awfully kind."

"Kindness itself," agreed Gamadge.

"And I was often so awfully low. I got to depend on her for sympathy, and all that kind of thing. And then Hunter seemed rather tired of me, used to be a little sarcastic about my never doing anything useful. She was driving back and forth to the hospital, and we used to—we had our talks away from the Farm. She wanted to be nice to me, and I got a sort of an idea that though she was fond of him, she was a little afraid of Hunter."

"She may well have been," said Gamadge.

"When I heard that gossip was going around, you can imagine what a state I was in. I cut out the meetings by the roadside, and finally I went and saw the old woman herself. She denied having said a thing, but she got off some cracks about Mrs. Star. That put me in a worse hole than ever. I had to confide in Leda. And what do you think she said?"

"Said she didn't care, and that it would be a fine cover-up for her Underground activities," murmured Gamadge.

"Yes, and that it didn't matter, since she was to go before long. So I used to drive her around, instead. Did Hunter actually listen in on Fanny and me?"

"Yes."

"But never said a word to Fanny? Thank goodness for that. She might have dropped me."

"Hunter wouldn't risk putting ideas into her head; he was too subtle a being to disturb their relationship in any way. But if he had really thought he was going to lose her, that would have been another matter. She never would have got away from him alive."

Craye said: "Scares you to think of. I hope she'll never know."

"She never will. Hunter kept her out of it—well out of it."

"Kept her out of it?" Craye was surprised.

"When he left me that night he went directly home, removed all signs that the telephone wires had been tampered with, got the receipt for the Radford securities—and other business papers—out of his safe; took his rifle down from the wall, and walked into the woods—where he was found next morning."

"Yes, I know. But—"

"The papers, and the Radford receipt, gave Ledwell the clear motive he wanted. They did more. The fact that Hunter didn't even try to save that seventy thousand for Fanny separates Fanny from the case almost as effectively as though she hadn't been married to him at all. People won't say she was the cause of it all."

"I did wonder why he fixed it so that she'd have to reimburse the Grobys."

"Phineas Hunter did nothing without good reason."

"But won't she be left very badly off?"

Macloud said in his gloomiest tone: "People who look like Fanny Hunter never are badly off for long."

Craye seemed to be made slightly restive by this remark. He took a cigarette from a box, thanked Gamadge for lighting it for him, and said after a moment: "I suppose she won't want to see any of us just yet. Remind her of the tragedy."

"She won't have a chance to see us," said Gamadge. "I told you she's with her people in New York. I took her down on Sunday."

"Yes, I know."

"Ledwell was very nice, didn't even make her wait for the inquest."

"How—how did she seem, Gamadge?"

"Oh—shattered. But she has lot of pluck; and—" Gamadge coughed—"I have reason to think that she never loved Hunter. Not what you and I mean by love, you know."

"It struck me that way," said Craye, repressing eagerness.

"She's very affectionate, you know," continued Gamadge, "and very pliant. She'll soon want to see her best friends."

"I'm to get up tomorrow," said Craye.

Mrs. Star came in with a tray of iced drinks. Macloud was introduced, blinked at sight of her pale beauty, and thereafter seemed unable to remove his eyes from her. Gamadge said: "I hope you've forgiven me, Mrs. Star, for letting you worry yourself half to death last Saturday night."

"Yes, I forgive you." She added, as she allowed him to take the tray from her, "And I hope you will forgive me for being so rude."

Gamadge looked unsmilingly at her across the tinkling glasses. "There were extenuating circumstances for us both."

"But I still say that you are a bad enemy."

"I don't particularly resent injuries to myself."

On the drive home Macloud was still glum. He said: "Fanny Hunter will marry him in a year."

"Why not? I don't want her to wear mourning for one unnecessary day. She won't take him for his money, Bob; she didn't marry Hunter for his money. It's not her fault that money seeks her out."

"I suppose it's not Craye's, or any man's fault, if he can't recognize the real thing when he sees it. That lovely creature worships him."

"He wants to worship Fanny."

Clara was on the porch waiting for them. Macloud, sinking down on the step and getting out his pipe, said that he didn't pity Gamadge for having to buy the place.

"Oh, the Grobys will let me off buying it now." Gamadge sat on the bench beside Clara. "Mrs. Groby called up to tell me so."

"I shouldn't want to be let off. Why don't you stay? Mountain Ridge is a long way off, and you'll have delightful friends at Stratfield."

"Macloud thinks Fanny will be there," Gamadge told his wife.

"I hope she will be." But Clara looked rather sadly at the tall trees opposite; behind them the hum of the waterfall was broken by small chucklings as its overflow of streamlets plunged into the pool.

"Clara wouldn't be happy here," said Gamadge.

"I would if you would."

Eli came along the road. When he stopped at the foot of

the path his Pharoah smile was broader than usual. "Too bad," he said.

Gamadge took his cigarette out of his mouth: "What's too bad?"

"Too bad you can't come back."

"To the cottage? Why can't we come back?"

"The reservation's making an offer for all this land, right down to the highway." Eli's arm swept in a semicircle from east to west.

Macloud remarked with a sardonic glance at Clara that her problem has been solved. "The tutelary gods have taken over," he said, "with Eli as their prophet."

"Yes." Gamadge leaned back and replaced his cigarette in his mouth. "I thought just now I heard them laughing."

ABOUT THE AUTHOR

ELIZABETH DALY was born in 1878 in New York City. The daughter of a judge and niece of the famous playwright and producer Augustin Daly, she grew up immersed in the world of literature and the theater. Miss Daly received her B.A. from Bryn Mawr College in 1901 and her M.A. from Columbia the following year. She later returned to Bryn Mawr as a reader in English and remained there for two years, adding to her duties the coaching and producing of amateur plays. Athough she began her literary career at the age of sixteen and published light verse and prose in various magazines, she did not write her first mystery novel until she was past sixty. In 1940, UNEXPECTED NIGHT was published and marked the first appearance of Henry Gamadge, her famous bibliophile detective. Miss Daly considered the detective novel at its best a high form of literature and didn't seek to write any other kind of fiction. Elizabeth Daly was a very popular writer in the United States as well as England, where Gamadge was dubbed "the American Peter Wimsey." One of her greatest fans was the grande dame of English mystery herself, Agatha Christie.

READ THESE GREAT BANTAM MYSTERIES BY TWO FINE WRITERS

Elizabeth Daly

Daly's sleuth is Henry Gamadge. Charming and genteel, dashingly attractive to women, Gamadge makes his home on the posh East Side of New York and makes his living as a consultant on old books, autographs, and inks. But he can find a missing body faster than a misplaced tome, decipher clues quicker than an ancient author's script, and has caught enough clever killers to fill a whole library of crime. Follow him in:

☐ THE WRONG WAY DOWN (23496-X • $2.50)
☐ THE BOOK OF THE CRIME (23811-6 • $2.50)
☐ EVIDENCE OF THINGS SEEN (23669-5 • $2.50)

Margery Allingham

Allingham introduces us to confidential investigator Albert Campion. A tall, thin man with overly large spectacles, he is deceptively unobtrusive when tracking down a killer and uncannily capable of predicting the deadly twists of a criminal's mind. He is unquestionably a gentleman, but even Lugg, his dauntless valet, and his friends at Scotland Yard don't know all the secrets in Campion's past—or the confidential cases he has covertly solved while in His Majesty's Service. He's quietly on the job in:

☐ TETHER'S END (23605-9 • $2.50)
☐ TRAITOR'S PURSE (23822-1 • $2.50)
Also read Margery Allingham's
☐ BLACK PLUMES (23590-7 • $2.50)

Buy all of these great Bantam mysteries wherever paperbacks are sold or use this handy coupon for ordering:

THE THRILLING AND MASTERFUL NOVELS OF
ROSS MACDONALD